1497

THE IMMORALIST

ANDRÉ GIDE

André Paul Guillaume Gide was born in Paris on 22 November 1869. His father, who died when he was eleven, was Professor of Law at the Sorbonne. An only child, Gide had an irregular and lonely upbringing and was educated in a Protestant secondary school in Paris and privately. He became devoted to literature and music, and began his literary career as an essayist, and then went on to poetry, biography, fiction, drama, criticism, reminiscence, and translation. By 1917 he had emerged as a prophet to French youth and his unortho-dox views were a source of endless debate and attack. In 1947 he was awarded the Nobel Prize for Literature and in 1948, as a distinguished foreigner, was given an honorary degree at Oxford. He married his cousin in 1892; he died in Paris in 1951 at the age of eighty-one. Gide's best-known works in England are *Strait is the Gate* (*La Porte Étroite*), the first novel he wrote, which was published in France in 1909; *The Coiners* (*Les Faux-Monnayeurs*) published in 1926; and the famous *Journals* covering his life from 1889 to 1949 and pub-lished in four volumes.

Cover portrait of André Gide from a lithograph by Marie Laurencion.

ANDRÉ GIDE

THE IMMORALIST

TRANSLATED BY
Dorothy Bussy

I will praise thee;
for I am fearfully and wonderfully made
PSALM CXXXIX: 14

PENGUIN BOOKS

Penguin Books Ltd, Harmondsworth, Middlesex
AUSTRALIA: Penguin Books Pty Ltd, 762 Whitehorse Road,
Mitcham, Victoria

—

L'Immoraliste first published 1902
This translation first published by Cassell 1930
Published in Penguin Books 1960
Reprinted 1961

—

Made and printed in Great Britain
by C. Nicholls & Company Ltd

TO
MY COMRADE AND FELLOW-TRAVELLER
Henri Ghéon

PREFACE

I PRESENT this book for what it is worth – a fruit filled with bitter ashes, like those colocynths of the desert that grow in a parched and burning soil. All they can offer to your thirst is a still more cruel fierceness – yet lying on the golden sand they are not without a beauty of their own.

If I had held my hero up as an example, it must be admitted that my success would have been small. The few readers who were disposed to interest themselves in Michel's adventure did so only to reprobate him with all the superiority of their kind hearts. It was not in vain that I had adorned Marceline with so many virtues; they could not forgive Michel for not preferring her to himself.

If I had intended this book to be an indictment of Michel, I should have succeeded as little, for no one was grateful to me for the indignation he felt against my hero; it was as though he felt this indignation in spite of me; it overflowed from Michel on to myself; I seemed indeed within an ace of being confounded with him.

But I intended to make this book as little an indictment as an apology and took care to pass no judgement. The public nowadays will not forgive an author who, after relating an action, does not declare himself either for or against it; more than this, during the very course of the drama they want him to take sides, pronounce in favour either of Alceste or Philinte, of Hamlet or Ophelia, of Faust or Margaret, of Adam or Jehovah. I do not indeed claim that neutrality (I was going to say 'indecision') is the certain mark of a great mind; but I believe that many great minds have been very loath to ... conclude – and that to state a problem clearly is not to suppose it solved in advance.

It is with reluctance that I use the word 'problem' here. To tell the truth, in art there are no problems – that are not sufficiently solved by the work of art itself.

If by 'problem' one means 'drama', shall I say that the one recounted in this book, though the scene of it is laid in my hero's soul, is nevertheless too general to remain circumscribed in his individual adventure. I do not pretend to have invented this 'problem'; it existed before my book; whether Michel triumph or succumb, the 'problem' will continue to exist, and the author has avoided taking either triumph or defeat for granted.

If certain distinguished minds have refused to see in this drama anything but the exposition of a special case, and in its hero anything but a sufferer from disease, if they have failed to recognize that ideas of very urgent import and very general interest may nevertheless be found in it – the fault lies neither in those ideas nor in that drama, but in the author – in his lack of skill, I should say – though he has put into this book all his passion and all his care, though he has watered it with many tears. But the real interest of a work and the interest taken in it by an ephemeral public are two very different things. A man may, I think, without much conceit, take the risk of not arousing immediate interest in interesting things – he may even prefer this to exciting a momentary delight in a public greedy only for sweets and trifles.

For the rest, I have not tried to prove anything, but only to paint my picture well and to set it in a good light.

Sidi B. M. 30th July 189–

YES, *My Dear Brother, of course, as you supposed, Michel has confided in us. Here is his story. You asked me to let you have it and I promised to; but now at the last moment I hesitate to send it and the oftener I re-read it the more dreadful it seems. Oh, what, I wonder, will you think of our friend? What, for that matter, do I think of him myself? ... Are we simply to reprobate him and deny the possibility of turning to good account faculties so manifestly cruel? But I fear there are not a few among us today who would be bold enough to recognize their own features in this tale. Will it be possible to invent some way of employing all this intelligence and strength? Or must they be altogether outlawed?*

In what way can Michel serve society? I admit I cannot guess ... He must have some occupation. Will the position and the power you have so deservedly attained enable you to find one? Make haste. Michel is still capable of devotion. Yes, he is so still. But it will soon be only to himself.

I am writing to you under a sky of flawless blue; during the twelve days that Denis, Daniel, and myself have been here, there has not been a single cloud nor the slightest diminution of sunshine. Michel says the weather has been of crystalline clearness for the last two months.

I am neither sad nor cheerful; the air here fills one with a kind of vague excitement and induces a state as far removed from cheerfulness as it is from sorrow; perhaps it is happiness.

We are staying with Michel; we are anxious not to leave him; you will understand why when you have read these pages;

so we shall await your reply here, in his house; lose no time about it.

You know what ties of friendship bound Michel, Denis, Daniel, and myself together — a friendship which was strong even in our school days, but which every year grew stronger. A kind of pact was concluded between us four — at the first summons of any one of us the other three were to hasten. So when I received that mysterious signal of alarm from Michel, I immediately informed Daniel and Denis, and we all three let everything go and set out.

It is three years since we last saw Michel. He had married and gone travelling with his wife, and at the time of his last stay in Paris, Denis was in Greece, Daniel in Russia, and I, as you know, looking after our sick father. We were not, however, without news, though the account given of him by Silas and Will, who saw him at that time, was, to say the least, surprising. He was no longer the learned Puritan of old days, whose behaviour was made awkward by his very earnestness, whose clear and simple gaze had so often checked the looseness of our talk. He was . . . but why forestall what his story will tell you?

Here is his story then, just as Denis, Daniel, and I heard it. Michel told it us on his terrace, as we were lying beside him in the dark and the starlight. At the end of his tale we saw day rising over the plain. Michel's house looks down on it and on the village which is not far off. In the hot weather and with all its crops reaped, this plain looks like the desert.

Michel's house, though poor and quaint-looking, is charming. In winter it would be cold, for there is no glass in the windows — or rather, there are no windows, but huge holes in the walls. It is so fine that we sleep out of doors on mats.

Let me add that we had a good journey out. We arrived here one evening, gasping with heat, intoxicated with novelty, after *having barely stopped on the way, first at Algiers and then at Constantine. At Constantine we took a second train to Sidi B. M., where a little cart was waiting for us. The road comes to an end some way from the village, which is perched on the top of a rock, like certain little hill-towns in Umbria. We climbed up on foot; two mules took our luggage. Approached by the road, Michel's house is the first in the village. It is surrounded by the low walls of a garden – or rather, an enclosure, in which there grow three stunted pomegranate-trees and a superb oleander. A little Kabyle boy ran away at the sight of us and scrambled over the wall without more ado.*

Michel showed no signs of pleasure as he welcomed us; he was very simple and seemed afraid of any demonstrations of tenderness; but on the threshold, he stopped and kissed each one of us gravely.

Until night came we barely exchanged a dozen words. An almost excessively frugal dinner was laid for us in a drawing-room where the decorations were so sumptuous that we were astonished by them though they were afterwards explained by Michel's story. Then he served us coffee, which he made a point of preparing himself; and afterwards we went up on to the terrace, where the view stretched away into infinity, and all three of us like Job's comforters sat down and waited, watching and admiring the day's abrupt decline over the incandescent plain.

When it was night Michel said:

FIRST PART

I

My dear friends, I knew you were faithful. You have answered my summons as quickly as I should have answered yours. And yet three years have gone by without your seeing me. May your friendship, which has been so proof against absence, be equally proof against the story I am going to tell you. For it was solely to see you, solely that you might listen to me, that I called upon you so suddenly and made you take this journey to my distant abode. The only help I wish for is this – to talk to you. For I have reached a point in my life beyond which I cannot go. Not from weariness though. But I can no longer understand things. I want ... I want to talk, I tell you. To know how to free oneself is nothing; the arduous thing is to know what to do with one's freedom. Let me speak of myself; I am going to tell you my life simply, without modesty and without pride, more simply than if I were talking to myself. Listen:

The last time we saw each other, I remember, was in the neighbourhood of Angers, in the little country church in which I was married. There were very few people at my wedding, and the presence of real friends turned this commonplace function into something touching. I felt that others were moved, and that in itself was enough to move me. After we left the church, you joined us at my bride's house for a short meal, at which there was neither noise nor laughter; then she and I drove away in a hired carriage, according to the custom by which we always have to associate the idea of a wedding with the vision of a railway station.

I knew my wife very little and thought, without being much distressed by it, that she knew me no better. I had married her without being in love, largely in order to please my father, who, as he lay dying, felt anxious at leaving me alone. I loved my father dearly; engrossed by his last illness, I had thought of nothing else all through that melancholy time but how to make his end easier; and so I pledged my life before I knew what the possibilities of life were. Our betrothal took place at my dying father's bedside, without laughter but not without a certain grave joy, so great was the peace it brought him. If, as I say, I did not love my betrothed, at any rate, I had never loved any other woman. This seemed to me sufficient to secure our happiness; and I thought I was giving her the whole of myself, without having any knowledge of what that self was. She was an orphan as I was, and lived with her two brothers. Her name was Marceline; she was barely twenty; I was four years older.

I have said I did not love her – at any rate, I felt for her nothing of what is generally known as love, but I loved her, if that word may cover a feeling of tenderness, a sort of pity, and a considerable measure of esteem. She was a Catholic and I a Protestant ... but, thought I, so little of a Protestant! The priest accepted me; I accepted the priest; it all went off without a hitch.

My father was what is called an 'atheist' – at least so I suppose, for a kind of invincible shyness, which I imagined he shared, had always made it impossible for

14

me to talk to him about his beliefs. The grave Hugue-
not teaching which my mother had given me had
slowly faded from my mind together with the image of
her beauty; you know I was young when I lost her. I
did not then suspect how great a hold the early moral
lessons of our childhood take of one, nor what marks
they leave upon the mind. That kind of austerity for
which a taste had been left in me by my mother's way
of bringing me up, I now applied wholly to my studies.
I was fifteen when I lost her; my father took me in
hand, looked after me, and himself instructed me with
passionate eagerness. I already knew Latin and Greek
well; under him I quickly learnt Hebrew, Sanskrit, and
finally Persian and Arabic. When I was about twenty I
had been so intensively forced that he actually made me
his collaborator. It amused him to claim me as his equal
and he wanted to show me he was right. *The Essay on
Phrygian Cults* which appeared under his name was in
reality my work; he scarcely read it over; nothing he
had written ever brought him so much praise. He was
delighted. As for me I was a little abashed by the success
of this deception. But my reputation was made. The
most learned scholars treated me as their colleague. I
smile now at all the honours that were paid me . . . And
so I reached the age of twenty-five, having barely cast a
glance at anything but books and ruins, and knowing
nothing of life; I spent all my fervour in my work. I
loved a few friends (you were among them), but it was
not so much my friends I loved as friendship – it was a
craving for high-mindedness that made my devotion to
them so great; I cherished in myself each and all of my
fine feelings. For the rest, I knew my friends as little as
I knew myself. The idea that I might have lived a

different existence or that anyone could possibly live differently never for a moment crossed my mind.

My father and I were satisfied with simple things; we both of us spent so little that I reached the age of twenty-five without knowing that we were rich. I imagined, without giving it much thought, that we had just enough to live on. And the habits of economy I had acquired with my father were so great that I felt almost uncomfortable when I learned that we had a great deal more. I was so careless about such matters that even after my father's death, though I was his sole heir, I failed to realize the extent of my fortune; I did so only when our marriage settlements were being drawn up, and at the same time I learned that Marceline brought me next to nothing.

And another thing I was ignorant of – even more important perhaps – was that I had very delicate health. How should I have known this, when I had never put it to the test? I had colds from time to time and neglected them. The excessive tranquillity of the life I led weakened, while at the same time it protected me. Marceline, on the contrary, seemed strong – that she was stronger than I we were very soon to learn.

*

On our wedding-day, we went straight to Paris and slept in my apartment, where two rooms had been got ready for us. We stayed in Paris only just long enough to do some necessary shopping, then took the train to Marseille and embarked at once for Tunis.

So many urgent things to be done, so many bewildering events following each other in too rapid succession, the unavoidable agitation of my wedding coming so soon after the more genuine emotion caused by my father's death – all of this had left me exhausted. It was only on the boat that I was able to realize how tired I was. Up till then, every occupation, while increasing my fatigue, had distracted me from feeling it. The enforced leisure on board ship at last enabled me to reflect. For the first time, so it seemed to me.

It was for the first time too that I had consented to forgo my work for any length of time. Up till then I had only allowed myself short holidays. A journey to Spain with my father shortly after my mother's death had, it is true, lasted over a month; another to Germany, six weeks; there were others too, but they had all been student's journeys; my father was never to be distracted from his own particular researches; when I was not accompanying him, I used to read. And yet, we had hardly left Marseille, when memories came back to me of Granada and Seville, of a purer sky, of franker shadows, of dances, of laughter, of songs. That is what we are going to find, I thought. I went up on to the deck and watched Marseille disappearing in the distance.

Then, suddenly, it occurred to me that I was leaving Marceline a little too much to herself.

She was sitting in the bow; I drew near, and for the first time really looked at her.

Marceline was very pretty. You saw her, so you know. I reproached myself for not having noticed it sooner. I had known her too long to see her with any freshness of vision; our families had been friends for ages; I had seen her grow up; I was accustomed to her grace ... For the first time now I was struck with astonishment, it seemed to me so great.

She wore a big veil floating from a simple black straw hat; she was fair, but did not look delicate. Her bodice and skirt were made of the same material – a Scotch plaid which we had chosen together. I had not wanted the gloom of my mourning to overshadow her.

She felt I was looking at her and turned towards me ... until then I had paid her only the necessary official attentions; I replaced love as best I could by a kind of frigid gallantry, which I saw well enough she found rather tiresome; perhaps at that moment Marceline felt I was looking at her for the first time in a different way. She in her turn looked fixedly at me; then, very tenderly, smiled. I sat down beside her without speaking. I had lived up to then for myself alone, or at any rate in my own fashion; I had married without imagining I should find in my wife anything different from a comrade, without thinking at all definitely that my life might be changed by our union. And now at last I realized that the monologue had come to an end.

We were alone on deck. She held up her face and I gently pressed her to me; she raised her eyes; I kissed her on the eyelids and suddenly felt as I kissed her an unfamiliar kind of pity, which took hold of me so violently that I could not restrain my tears.

'What is it, dear?' said Marceline.

We began to talk. What she said was so charming that it delighted me. I had picked up in one way or another a few ideas on women's silliness. That evening, in her presence, it was myself I thought awkward and stupid.

So the being to whom I had attached my life had a real and individual life of her own! The importance of this thought woke me up several times during the night; several times I sat up in my berth in order to look at Marceline, my wife, asleep in the berth below.

The next morning the sky was splendid; the sea almost perfectly calm. A few leisurely talks lessened our shyness still more. Marriage was really beginning. On the morning of the last day of October we landed in Tunis.

*

I intended to stay there only a few days. I will confess my folly; in so new a country nothing attracted me except Carthage and a few Roman ruins – Timgad, about which Octave had spoken to me, the mosaics of Sousse, and above all the amphitheatre of El Djem, which I decided we must visit without delay. We had first to get to Sousse, and from Sousse take the mail diligence; between there and here I was determined to think nothing worth my attention.

And yet Tunis surprised me greatly. At the touch of new sensations, certain portions of me awoke – certain sleeping faculties, which, from not having as yet been used, had kept all their mysterious freshness. But I was more astonished, more bewildered than amused, and what pleased me most was Marceline's delight.

My fatigue in the meantime was growing greater every day; but I should have thought it shameful to give in to it. I had a bad cough and a curious feeling of discomfort in the upper part of my chest. We were going towards the south, I thought; the heat will put me to rights again.

The Sfax diligence leaves Sousse at eight o'clock in the evening and passes through El Djem at one o'clock in the morning. We had engaged coupé places; I expected to find an uncomfortable shandrydan; the seats,

however, were fairly commodious. But oh, the cold!
... We were both lightly clad and, with a kind of child-
ish confidence in the warmth of southern climes, had
taken no wrap with us but a single shawl. As soon as
we were out of Sousse and the shelter of its hills, the
wind began to blow. It leaped over the plain in great
bounds, howling, whistling, coming in by every chink
of the door and windows – impossible to protect oneself from it! We were both chilled to the bone when we
arrived, and I was exhausted as well by the jolting of
the carriage and by my horrible cough, which shook
me even worse. What a night! When we got to El
Djem, there was no inn, nothing but a frightful native
bordj. What was to be done? The diligence was going
on; the village was asleep; the lugubrious mass of the
ruins lowered dimly through the dark immensity of the
night; dogs were howling. We went into a room whose
walls and floor were made of mud and in which stood
two wretched beds. Marceline was shivering with cold,
but here at any rate we were out of the wind.

The next day was a dismal one. We were surprised on
going out to see a sky that was one unrelieved grey.
The wind was still blowing, but less violently than the
night before. The diligence passed through again only
in the evening ... It was a dismal day, I tell you. I went
over the amphitheatre in a few minutes and found it
disappointing; I thought it actually ugly under that
dreary sky. Perhaps my fatigue added to my feeling of
tedium. Towards the middle of the day, as I had nothing else to do, I went back to the ruins and searched
in vain for inscriptions on the stones. Marceline found
a place that was sheltered from the wind and sat
reading an English book, which by good luck

she had brought with her. I went and sat beside her.

'What a melancholy day!' I said. 'Aren't you bored?'

'Not particularly. I am reading.'

'What made us come to such a place? I hope you are not cold, are you?'

'Not so very. Are you? Oh, you must be. How pale you are!'

'No, oh no!'

At night, the wind began again as violently as ever ... At last the diligence arrived. We started.

No sooner did the jolting begin than I felt shattered. Marceline, who was very tired, had gone to sleep almost at once on my shoulder. My cough will wake her, I thought, and freeing myself very, very gently, I propped her head against the side of the carriage. In the meantime I had stopped coughing; yes; I had begun to spit instead; this was something new; I brought it up without an effort; it came in little jerks at regular intervals; the sensation was so odd that at first it almost amused me, but I was soon disgusted by the peculiar taste it left in my mouth. My handkerchief was very soon used up. My fingers were covered with it. Should I wake up Marceline?

... Fortunately I thought of a large silk foulard she was wearing tucked into her belt. I took possession of it quietly. The spitting, which I no longer tried to keep back, came more abundantly and I was extraordinarily relieved by it. It is the end of my cold, I thought. Then, there suddenly came over me a feeling of extreme weakness; everything began to spin round and I thought I was going to faint. Should I wake her up? ... No, shame! ... (My puritanical childhood has left me, I think, a hatred of any surrender to bodily weakness – cowardice, I call it.) I controlled myself, made a desperate effort, and finally conquered my giddiness ... I felt as if I were at sea again, and the noise of the wheels turned into the sound of the waves ... But I had stopped spitting.

Then I sank, overpowered, into a sort of sleep.

When I emerged from it, the sky was already filling with dawn. Marceline was still asleep. We were just getting to Sousse. The foulard I was holding in my hand was dark-coloured, so that at first I saw nothing; but when I took out my handkerchief, I saw with stupefaction that it was soaked with blood.

My first thought was to hide the blood from Marceline. But how? I was covered with it; it seemed to be everywhere; on my fingers especially ... My nose might perhaps have been bleeding ... That's it! If she asks me, I shall say my nose has been bleeding.

Marceline was still asleep. We drew up at the Sousse hotel. She had to get down first and saw nothing. Our two rooms had been kept for us. I was able to dart into mine and wash away every trace of blood. Marceline had seen nothing.

I was feeling very weak, however, and ordered some tea to be brought. And as she was pouring it out, a little pale herself, but very calm and smiling, a kind of irritation seized me to think she had not had the sense to see anything. I felt indeed that I was being unjust, and said to myself that she saw nothing only because I had hidden it from her so cleverly; but I couldn't help it – the feeling grew in me like an instinct, filled me ... and at last it became too strong; I could contain myself

22

no longer; the words slipped out, as though absent-mindedly:

'I spat blood last night.'

She did not utter a sound; she simply turned much paler, tottered, tried to save herself, and fell heavily to the ground.

I sprang to her in a sort of fury: 'Marceline! Marceline!' What on earth had I done? Wasn't it enough for *me* to be ill? But, as I have said, I was very weak; I was on the point of fainting myself. I managed, however, to open the door and call. Someone hurried to our help.

I remember that I had a letter of introduction to an officer in the town, and on the strength of this I sent for the regimental doctor.

Marceline in the meantime had recovered herself and settled down at my bedside, where I lay shivering with fever. The doctor came and examined us both; there was nothing the matter with Marceline, he declared, and she had not been hurt by her fall; *I* was seriously ill; he refused to give a definite opinion and promised to come back before evening.

He came back, smiled at me, talked to me and pre-scribed various remedies. I realized that he gave me up for lost. Shall I confess that I felt not the least shock? I was very tired, I simply let myself go. After all, what had life to offer? I had worked faithfully to the end, resolutely and passionately done my duty. The rest ... oh! what did it matter? thought I, with a certain ad-miration of my own stoicism. What really pained me was the ugliness of my surroundings. 'This hotel room is frightful,' I thought, and looked at it. Suddenly it occurred to me that in a like room next door was my wife, Marceline; and I heard her speaking. The doctor had not gone; he was talking to her, he was studiously lowering his voice. A little time went by – I must have slept . . .

When I woke up, Marceline was there. I could see she had been crying. I did not care for life enough to pity myself; but the ugliness of the place vexed me; my eyes rested on her with a pleasure that was almost voluptuous.

She was sitting by me writing. I thought she looked very pretty. I saw her fasten up several letters. Then she got up, drew near my bed, and took my hand tenderly.

'How are you feeling now?' she asked. I smiled and said sadly: 'Shall I get better?'

But she answered at once, 'You *shall* get better' with such passionate conviction that it almost brought conviction to me too, and there came over me a kind of confused feeling of all that life might mean, of Marceline's own love – a vague vision of such apathetic beauties that the tears started from my eyes and I wept long and helplessly without trying or wanting to stop.

With what loving violence she managed to get me away from Sousse! How charmingly she protected me, helped me, nursed me! From Sousse to Tunis, from Tunis to Constantine, Marceline was admirable. It was at Biskra that I was to get well. Her confidence was perfect; never for a single moment did her zeal slacken. She settled everything, arranged the starts, engaged the rooms. It was not in her power, alas! to make the journey less horrible. Several times I thought I should have to stop and give up. I sweated mortally; I gasped for breath; at times I lost consciousness. At the end of the third day, I arrived at Biskra more dead than alive.

2

WHY speak of those first days? What remains of them? Their frightful memory has no tongue. I lost all knowledge of who or where I was. I can only see Marceline, my wife, my life, bending over the bed where I lay agonizing. I know that her passionate care, her love, alone saved me. One day, at last, like a shipwrecked mariner who catches sight of land, I felt a gleam of life revisit me; I was able to smile at Marceline. Why should I recall all this? What is important is that Death had touched me, as people say, with its wing. What is important is that I came to think it a very astonishing thing to be alive, that every day shone for me, an unhoped-for light. Before, thought I, I did not understand I was alive. The thrilling discovery of life was to be mine.

The day came when I was able to get up. I was utterly enchanted by our home. It was almost nothing but a terrace. What a terrace! My room and Marceline's opened out on to it; at the further end it was continued over roofs. From the highest part, one saw palm-trees above the houses; and above the palm-trees, the desert. On the other side, the terrace adjoined the public gardens and was shaded by the branches of the nearest cassias; lastly, it ran along one side of the courtyard – a small, regular courtyard, planted regularly with six palm-trees – and came to an end with the staircase that led down to the courtyard. My room was spacious and airy; the walls were bare and whitewashed; a little door led to Marceline's room; a large door with glass panes opened on to the terrace.

There the hourless days slipped by. How often in my solitude those slow-slipping days come back to me! ... Marceline sits beside me. She is reading, or sewing, or writing. I am doing nothing – just looking at her. O Marceline! Marceline! ... I look, I see the sun; I see the shadow; I see the line of shadow moving; I have so little to think of that I watch it. I am still very weak; my breathing is very bad; everything tires me – even reading; besides, what should I read? Existing is occupation enough.

*

One morning Marceline came in laughing.

'I have brought you a friend,' she said, and I saw come in behind her a little dark-complexioned Arab. His name was Bachir and he had large silent eyes that looked at me. They made me feel embarrassed, and that was enough to tire me. I said nothing, only looked cross. The child, disconcerted by the coldness of my reception, turned to Marceline and, with the coaxing grace of a little animal, nestled up against her, took her hand and kissed it, showing his bare arms as he did so. I noticed that under his thin, white gandourah and patched burnous, he was naked.

'Come, sit down there,' said Marceline, who had noticed my shyness. 'Amuse yourself quietly.'

The little fellow sat down on the floor, took a knife and a piece of djerid wood out of the hood of his burnous, and began to slice at it. I think it was a whistle he was trying to make.

After a little time, I ceased to feel uncomfortable. I looked at him; he seemed to have forgotten where he was. His feet were bare: he had charmingly turned ankles and wrists. He handled his wretched knife with amusing dexterity ... Was this really going to interest me? ... His hair was shaved Arab fashion; he wore a shabby chechia on his head with a hole in the place of the tassel. His gandourah, which had slipped down a little, showed his delicate little shoulder. I wanted to touch it. I bent down; he turned round and smiled at me. I signed to him to pass me his whistle, took it, and pretended to admire it. After a time he said he must go. Marceline gave him a cake and I a penny.

The next day, for the first time, I felt dull. I seemed to be expecting something. Expecting what? I was list-less, restless. At last I could resist no longer.

'Isn't Bachir coming this morning, Marceline?'

'If you like, I'll fetch him.'

She left me and went out; after a little she came back alone. What kind of thing had illness made me that I should have felt inclined to cry at seeing her return without Bachir?

'It was too late,' she said, 'the children had come out of school and dispersed. Some of them are really charming. I think they all know me now.'

'Well, at any rate, try and get him to come tomor-row.'

Next morning Bachir came back. He sat down in the same way he had done two days before, took out his knife and tried to carve his bit of wood, but it was too hard for him and he finally managed to stick the blade into his thumb. I shuddered with horror, but he laughed, held out his hand for me to see the glistening cut and looked amused at the sight of his blood run-ning. When he laughed, he showed very white teeth; he licked his cut complacently and his tongue was as pink as a cat's. Ah! how well he looked! That was what I had fallen in love with – his health. The health of that little body was a beautiful thing.

The day after he brought some marbles. He wanted to make me play. Marceline was out or she would have prevented me. I hesitated and looked at Bachir; the little fellow seized my arm, put the marbles into my hand, forced me. The attitude of stooping made me very breathless, but I tried to play all the same. Bachir's pleasure charmed me. At last, however, it was too much for me. I was in a profuse perspiration. I pushed aside the marbles and dropped into an armchair. Bachir, somewhat disturbed, looked at me.

'Ill?' said he sweetly; the quality of his voice was exquisite. Marceline came back at that moment.

'Take him away,' I said, 'I am tired this morning.' A few hours later I had an haemorrhage. It was while I was taking a laborious walk up and down the terrace; Marceline was busy in her room and fortunately saw nothing. My breathlessness had made me take a deeper respiration than usual and the thing had suddenly come. It had filled my mouth . . . But it was no longer bright, clear blood as on the first occasion. It was a frightful great clot which I spat on to the ground in disgust.

I took a few tottering steps. I was horribly upset. I was frightened; I was angry. For up till then I had thought that, step by step, recovery was on the way, and that I had nothing to do but wait for it. This brutal accident had thrown me back. The strange thing is that the first haemorrhage had not affected me so much. I now remembered it had left me almost calm. What was the reason of my fear, my horror now? Alas! it was because I had begun to love life.

I returned on my steps, bent down, found the clot, and with a piece of straw picked it up and put it on my handkerchief. It was hideous, almost black in colour, sticky, slimy, horrible ... I thought of Bachir's beautiful, brilliant flow of blood ... And suddenly I was seized with a desire, a craving, something more furious and more imperious than I had ever felt before – to live! I want to live! I *will* live. I clenched my teeth, my hands, concentrated my whole being in this wild, grief-stricken endeavour towards existence.

The day before, I had received a letter from T ..., written in answer to Marceline's anxious inquiries; it was full of medical advice; T ... had even accompanied his letter with one of two little popular medical pamphlets and a book of a more technical nature, which for that reason seemed to me more serious. I had read the letter carelessly and the printed matter not at all; in the first place I was set against the pamphlets because of their likeness to the moral tracts that used to tease me in my childhood; and then too every kind of advice was irksome to me; and besides, I did not think that *Advice to Tuberculous Patients* or *How to Cure Tuberculosis* in any way concerned me. I did not think I was tuberculous. I inclined to attribute my first haemorrhage to a different cause; or rather, to tell the truth, I did not attribute it to anything; I avoided thinking of it, hardly thought of it at all, and considered myself, if not altogether cured, at least very nearly so ... I read the letter; I devoured the book, the pamphlets. Suddenly, with shocking clearness, it became evident to me that I had not treated myself properly. Hitherto, I had let myself live passively, trusting to the vaguest of hopes; suddenly I perceived my life was attacked – attacked in its very centre. An active host of enemies was living within me. I listened to them; I spied on them; I felt them. I should not vanquish them without a struggle . . . and I added half aloud, as if better to convince myself, 'It is a matter of will.'

I put myself in a state of hostility.

Evening was closing in; I planned my strategy. For some time to come, my recovery was to be my one and only concern; my duty was my health; I must think good; I must call right everything that was salutary to me, forget everything that did not contribute to my cure. Before the evening meal, I had decided on my measures with regard to breathing, exercise, and nourishment.

We used to take our meals in a sort of little kiosk that was surrounded by the terrace on all sides. We were alone, quiet, far from everything, and the intimacy of our meals was delightful. An old Negro used to bring us our food, which was tolerable, from a neighbouring hotel. Marceline superintended the menus, ordered one dish or rejected another . . . Not having much appetite as a rule, I did not mind particularly when the dishes were a failure or the menu insufficient. Marceline, who was herself a small eater, did not know, did not realize that I was not taking enough food. To eat a great deal was the first of my new resolutions. I intended to put it into execution that very evening. I was not able to. We had some sort of uneatable hash, and then a bit of roast meat which was absurdly overdone.

My irritation was so great that I vented it upon Marceline and let myself go in a flood of intemperate words. I blamed her; to listen to me, it was as though she were responsible for the badness of the food. This slight delay in starting on the régime I had decided to adopt seemed of the gravest importance; I forgot the preceding days; the failure of this one meal spoiled everything. I persisted obstinately. Marceline had to go into the town to buy a tin or a jar of anything she could find.

She soon came back with a little terrine, of which I devoured almost the whole contents, as though to prove to us both how much I was in need of more food.

That same evening we settled on the following plan: the meals were to be much better and there were to be more of them – one every three hours, beginning as early as half past six in the morning. An abundant provision of every kind of tinned food was to supplement the deficiencies of the hotel menus.

I could not sleep that night, so excited was I by the vision of my future virtues. I was, I think, a little feverish; there was a bottle of mineral water beside me; I drank a glass, two glasses; the third time, I drank out of the bottle itself and emptied it at a draught. I strengthened my will as one strengthens one's memory by revising a lesson; I instructed my hostility, directed it against all and sundry; I was to fight with everything; my salvation depended on myself alone.

At last I saw the night begin to pale; another day had dawned.

It had been my night of vigil before the battle.

The next day was Sunday. Must I confess that so far I had paid very little attention to Marceline's religious beliefs? Either from indifference or delicacy, it seemed to me that they were no business of mine; and then I did not attach much importance to them. That morning Marceline went to Mass. When she came back, she told me she had been praying for me. I looked at her fixedly and then said as gently as I could:

'You mustn't pray for me, Marceline.'

'Why not?' she asked, a little troubled.

'I don't want favours.'

'Do you reject the help of God?'

'He would have a right to my gratitude afterwards. It entails obligations. I don't like them.'

To all appearances we were trifling, but we made no mistake as to the importance of our words.

'You will not get well all by yourself, my poor dear,' she sighed.

'If so, it can't be helped.' Then, seeing how unhappy she looked, I added less roughly:

'You will help me.'

3

I AM going to speak at length of my body. I shall speak of it so much you will think at first I have forgotten my soul. This omission, as I tell you my story, is intentional; out there, it was a fact. I had not strength enough to keep up a double life. 'I will think of the spirit and that side of things later,' I said to myself, '– when I get better'.

I was still far from being well. The slightest thing put me into a perspiration; the slightest thing gave me a cold; my breath was short; sometimes I had a little fever, and often, from early morning, oppressed by a dreadful feeling of lassitude, I remained prostrate in an armchair, indifferent to everything, self-centred, solely occupied in trying to breathe properly. I breathed laboriously, methodically, carefully; my expiration came in two jerks which, with the greatest effort of my will, I could only partially control; for a long time after that, I still had need of all my attention to avoid this.

But what troubled me most was my morbid sensibility to changes of temperature. I think, when I come to reflect on it today, that, in addition to my illness, I was suffering from a general nervous derangement. I cannot otherwise explain a series of phenomena which it seems to me impossible to attribute entirely to a simple condition of tuberculosis. I was always either too hot or too cold; I put on a ridiculous number of clothes, and only stopped shivering when I began to perspire; then directly I took anything off, I shivered as soon as I stopped perspiring. Certain portions of my body would turn as cold as ice and, in spite of perspiration, felt like marble to the touch; nothing would warm them. I was so sensitive to cold that if a little water dropped on my feet while I was washing, it gave me a relapse; I was equally sensitive to heat ... This sensibility I kept and still keep, but now it gives me exquisite enjoyment. Any very keen sensibility may, I believe, according as the organism is robust or weakly, become a source of delight or discomfort. Everything which formerly distressed me is now a delicious pleasure.

I do not know how I had managed to sleep up till then with my windows shut; in accordance with T...'s advice, I now tried keeping them open at night; a little at first; soon I flung them wide; soon it became a habit, a need so great that directly the window was shut, I felt stifled. Later on, with what rapture was I to feel the night wind blow, the moon shine in upon me! ...

But I am eager to have done with these first stammerings after health. Indeed, thanks to constant attention, to pure air, to better food, I soon began to improve. Up till then, my breathlessness had made me dread the stairs and I had not dared to leave the terrace; in the last days of January I at last went down and ventured into the garden.

Marceline came with me, carrying a shawl. It was three o'clock in the afternoon. The wind, which is often violent in those parts and which I had found particularly unpleasant during the last few days, had dropped. The air was soft and charming.

The public gardens! ... A very wide path runs through the middle of them, shaded by two rows of that kind of very tall mimosa which out there is called cassia. Benches are placed in the shadow of the trees. A canalized river – one, I mean, that is not wide so much as deep, and almost straight – flows alongside the path; other smaller channels take the water from the river and convey it through the gardens to the plants; the thick, heavy-looking water is the same colour as the earth – the colour of pinkish, greyish clay. Hardly any foreigners walk here – only a few Arabs; as they pass out of the sunlight, their white cloaks take on the colour of the shade.

I felt an odd shiver come over me as I stepped into that strange shade; I wrapped my shawl tighter about me; but it was not an unpleasant sensation; on the contrary. We sat down on a bench. Marceline was silent. Some Arabs passed by; then came a troop of children. Marceline knew several of them; she signed to them and they came up to us. She told me some of their names; questions and answers passed, smiles, pouts, little jokes. It all rather irritated me and my feeling of embarrassment returned. I was tired and perspiring. But must I confess that what made me most uncomfortable was not the children's presence – it was Marceline's. Yes; however slightly, she was in my way. If I had got up, she would have followed me; if I had taken off my shawl, she would have wanted to carry it; if I had put it on again, she would have said, 'Are you cold?' And then, as to talking to the children, I didn't dare to before her; I saw that she had her favourites; I, in spite of myself, but deliberately, took more interest in the others.

'Let us go in,' I said at last. And I privately resolved to come back to the gardens alone.

The next day, she had to go out about ten o'clock; I took advantage of this. Little Bachir, who rarely failed to come of a morning, carried my shawl; I felt active, light-hearted. We were almost alone in the garden path. I walked slowly, sometimes sat down for a moment, then started off again. Bachir followed, chattering; as faithful and as obsequious as a dog. I reached a part of the canal where the washerwomen come down to wash; there was a flat stone placed in the middle of the stream, and upon it lay a little girl, face downwards, dabbling with her hand in the water; she was busy throwing little odds and ends of sticks and grass into the water and picking them out again. Her bare feet had dipped in the water; there were still traces of wet on them and there her skin showed darker. Bachir went up and spoke to her; she turned round, gave me a smile and answered Bachir in Arabic. 'She is my sister,' he explained; then he said his mother was coming to wash some clothes and that his little sister was waiting for her. She was called Rhadra in Arabic, which meant 'Green'. He said all this in a voice that was as charming, as clear, as childlike, as the emotion I felt in hearing it.

'She wants you to give her two sous,' he added.

I gave her fifty centimes and prepared to go on, when the mother, the washerwoman, came up. She was a magnificent, heavily built woman, with a high forehead tatooed in blue; she was carrying a basket of linen on her head and was like a Greek caryatid; like a caryatid too, she was simply draped in a wide piece of dark blue stuff, lifted at the girdle and falling straight to the feet.

As soon as she saw Bachir, she called out to him roughly. He made an angry answer; the little girl joined in and the three of them started a violent dispute. At last Bachir seemed defeated and explained that his mother wanted him that morning; he handed me my shawl sadly and I was obliged to go off by myself.

I had not taken twenty paces when my shawl began to feel unendurably heavy. I sat down, perspiring, on the first bench I came to. I hoped some other boy would come along and relieve me of my burden. The one who soon appeared and who offered to carry it of his own accord, was a big boy about fourteen years old, as black as a Sudanese and not in the least shy. His name was Ashour. I should have thought him handsome, but that he was blind in one eye. He liked talking; told me where the river came from, and that after running through the public gardens, it flowed into the oasis, which it traversed from end to end. As I listened to him, I forgot my fatigue. Charming as I thought Bachir, I know him too well by now, and I was glad of a change. I even promised myself to come to the gardens all alone another day and sit on a bench and wait for what some lucky chance might bring ...

After a few more short rests, Ashour and I arrived at my door. I wanted to invite him to come in, but I was afraid to, not knowing what Marceline would say.

I found her in the dining-room, busied over a very small boy, so frail and sickly looking that my first feeling was one of disgust rather than pity. Marceline said rather timidly:

'The poor little thing is ill.'

'It's not infectious, I hope. What's the matter with him?'

'I don't exactly know yet. He complains of feeling ill all over. He speaks very little French. When Bachir comes tomorrow, he will be able to interpret ... I am making him a little tea.'

Then, as if in excuse, and because I stood there without saying anything, 'I've known him a long time,' she added. 'I haven't dared bring him in before; I was afraid of tiring you, or perhaps vexing you.'

'Why in the world!' I cried. 'Bring in all the children you like, if it amuses you!' And I thought, with a little irritation at not having done so, that I might have perfectly well brought in Ashour.

And yet, as I thought this, I looked at my wife; how maternal and caressing she was! Her tenderness was so touching that the little fellow went off warm and comforted. I spoke of my walk and gently explained to Marceline why I preferred going out alone.

At that time, my nights were generally disturbed by my constantly waking with a start – either frozen with cold or bathed in sweat. That night was a very good one. I hardly woke up at all. The next morning, I was ready to go out by nine o'clock. It was fine; I felt rested, not weak, happy – or rather, amused. The air was calm and warm, but nevertheless, I took my shawl to serve as a pretext for making acquaintance with the boy who might turn up to carry it. I have said that the garden ran alongside our terrace, so that I reached it in a moment. It was with rapture I passed into its shade. The air was luminous. The cassias, whose flowers come very early, before their leaves, gave out a delicious scent – or was it from all around me that came the faint, strange perfume, which seemed to enter me by several senses at once and which so uplifted me? I was breathing more easily too, and so I walked more lightly; and yet at the first bench I sat down, but it was because I was excited – dazzled – rather than tired.

I looked. The shadows were transparent and mobile;

they did not fall upon the ground – seemed barely to rest on it. Light! Oh, light!

I listened. What did I hear? Nothing; everything; every sound amused me.

I remember a shrub some way off whose bark looked of such a curious texture that I felt obliged to go and feel it. My touch was a caress; it gave me rapture. I remember ... Was that the morning that was at last to give me birth?

I had forgotten I was alone, and sat on, expecting nothing, waiting for no one, forgetting the time. Up till that day, so it seemed to me, I had felt so little and thought so much that now I was astonished to find my sensations had become as strong as my thoughts.

I say, 'it *seemed* to me', for from the depths of my past childhood, there now awoke in me the glimmerings of a thousand lost sensations. The fact that I was once more aware of my senses enabled me to give them a half fearful recognition. Yes; my reawakened senses now remembered a whole ancient history of their own – recomposed for themselves a vanished past. They were alive! Alive! They had never ceased to live; they discovered that even during those early studious years they had been living their own latent, cunning life.

I met no one that day, and I was glad of it; I took out of my pocket a little Homer, which I had not opened since Marseille, re-read three lines of the *Odyssey* and learned them by heart; then, finding in their rhythm enough to satisfy me, I dwelled on them awhile with leisurely delight, shut the book, and sat still, trembling, more alive than I had thought it possible to be, my mind benumbed with happiness ...

4

IN the meantime, Marceline, who saw with delight that my health was at last improving, had after a few days begun telling me about the marvellous orchards of the oasis. She was fond of the open air and outdoor exercise. My illness left her enough spare time for long walks, from which she returned glowing with enthusiasm; so far she had not said much about them, as she did not dare invite me to go with her and was afraid of depressing me by an account of delights I was not yet fit to enjoy. But now that I was better, she counted on their attraction to complete my recovery. The pleasure I was again beginning to take in walking and looking about me tempted me to join her. And the next morning we set out together.

She led the way along a path so odd that I have never in any country seen its like. It meanders indolently between two fairly high mud walls; the shape of the gardens they enclose directs its leisurely course; sometimes it winds; sometimes it is broken; a sudden turning as you enter it and you lose your bearings; you cease to know where you came from or where you are going. The water of the river follows the path faithfully and runs alongside one of the walls; the walls are made of the same earth as the path – the same as that of the whole oasis – a pinkish or soft grey clay, which is turned a little darker by the water, which the burning sun crackles, which hardens in the heat and softens with the first shower, so that it becomes a plastic soil that keeps the imprint of every naked foot. Above the walls, palm-trees show. Wood-pigeons went flying into them as we came up. Marceline looked at me.

I forgot my discomfort and fatigue. I walked on in a sort of ecstasy, of silent joy, of elation of the senses and the flesh. At that moment there came a gentle breath of wind; all the palms waved and we saw the tallest of the trees bending; then the whole air grew calm again, and I distinctly heard, coming from behind the wall, the song of a flute. A breach in the wall; we went in.

It was a place full of light and shade; tranquil; it seemed beyond the touch of time; full of silence; full of rustlings – the soft noise of running water that feeds the palms and slips from tree to tree, the quiet call of the pigeons, the song of the flute the boy was playing. He was sitting, almost naked, on the trunk of a fallen palm-tree, watching a herd of goats; our coming did not disturb him; he did not move – stopped playing only for a moment.

I noticed during this brief pause that another flute was answering in the distance. We went on a little, then:

'It's no use going any further,' said Marceline; 'these orchards are all alike; possibly at the other end of the oasis they may be a little larger ...'

She spread the shawl on the ground. 'Sit down and rest,' she said.

How long did we stay there? I cannot tell. What mattered time? Marceline was near me; I lay down and put my head on her knees. The song of the flute flowed on, stopped from time to time, went on again, the sound of the water ... From time to time a goat baa'ed. I shut my eyes; I felt Marceline lay her cool hand on my forehead; I felt the burning sun, gently shaded by the palm-trees; I thought of nothing; what mattered thoughts? I *felt* extraordinarily ...

And from time to time there was another noise; I opened my eyes; a little wind was blowing in the palm-trees; it did not come down low enough to reach us – stirred only the highest branches.

The next morning, I returned to the same garden with Marceline; on the evening of the same day, I went back to it alone. The goatherd who played the flute was there. I went up to him; spoke to him. He was called Lassif, was only twelve years old, was a handsome boy. He told me the names of his goats, told me that the little canals are called seghias, they do not all run every day, he explained, the water, wisely and parsimoniously distributed, satisfies the thirst of the plants, and is then at once withdrawn. At the foot of each palm the ground is hollowed out into a small cup which holds water enough for the tree's needs; an ingenious system of sluices, which the boy worked for me to see, controls the water, conducts it wherever the ground is thirstiest.

The next day I saw a brother of Lassif's; he was a little older and not so handsome; he was called Lachmi. By means of the kind of ladder made in the trunk of the tree by the old stumps of excised palm leaves he climbed up to the top of a pollarded palm; then he came swiftly down again, showing a golden nudity beneath his floating garment. He brought down a little earthen gourd from the place where the head of the tree had been severed; it had been hung up near the fresh cut in order to collect the palm sap, from which the Arabs make a sweet wine they are extremely fond of. At

Lachmi's invitation, I tasted it; but I did not like its sickly, raw, syrupy taste.

The following days I went further; I saw other gardens, other goatherds and other goats. As Marceline had said, all these gardens were alike; and yet they were all different.

Sometimes Marceline would still come with me; but more often, as soon as we reached the orchards, I would leave her, persuade her that I was tired, that I wanted to sit down, that she must not wait for me, for she needed more exercise; so that she would finish the walk without me. I stayed behind with the children. I soon knew a great number of them; I had long conversations with them; I learned their games, taught them others, lost all my pennies at pitch and toss. Some of them used to come with me on my walks (every day I walked farther), showed me some new way home, took charge of my coat and my shawl when I happened to have them both with me. Before leaving the children, I used to distribute a handful of pennies among them; sometimes they would follow me, playing all the way, as far as my own door; and finally they would sometimes come in.

Then Marceline on her side brought in others. She brought the boys who went to school, whom she encouraged to work; when school broke up, the good little boys, the quiet little boys came in; those that I brought were different; but they made friends over their games. We took care always to have a store of syrups and sweetmeats on hand. Soon other boys came of their own accord, even uninvited. I remember each one of them; I can see them still . . .

*

Towards the end of January, the weather changed suddenly; a cold wind sprang up and my health immediately began to suffer. The great open space that separates the oasis from the town became impassable, and I was obliged once more to content myself with the public gardens. Then it began to rain – an icy rain, which covered the mountains on the far northern horizon with snow.

I spent those melancholy days beside the fire, gloomily, obstinately, fighting with my illness, which in this vile weather gained upon me. Lugubrious days! I could neither read nor work; the slightest effort brought on the most troublesome perspiration; fixing my thoughts exhausted me; directly I stopped paying attention to my breathing, I suffocated.

During those melancholy days the children were my only distraction. In the rainy weather, only the most familiar came in; their clothes were drenched; they sat round the fire in a circle. A long time would often go by without anything being said, I was too tired, too unwell to do anything but look at them; but the presence of their good health did me good. Those that Marceline petted were weakly, sickly, and too well behaved; I was irritated with her and with them and ended by keeping them at arm's length. To tell the truth, they frightened me.

One morning I had a curious revelation as to my own character; Moktir, the only one of my wife's protégés who did not irritate me (because of his good looks perhaps), was alone with me in my room; up till then, I had not cared much about him, but there was something strange, I thought, in the brilliant and sombre expression of his eyes. Some kind of inexplicable curiosity made me watch his movements. I was standing in front of the fire, my two elbows on the mantelpiece, apparently absorbed in a book; but, though I had my back turned to him, I could see what he was doing reflected in the glass. Moktir did not know I was watching him and thought I was immersed in my reading. I saw him go noiselessly up to a table where Marceline had laid her work and a little pair of scissors beside it, seize them furtively, and in a twinkling engulf them in the folds of his burnous. My heart beat quickly for a moment, but neither reason nor reflection could arouse in me the smallest feeling of indignation. More than that! I could not manage to persuade myself that the feeling that filled me at the sight was anything but joy.

When I had allowed Moktir ample time for robbing me, I turned round again and spoke to him as if nothing had happened.

Marceline was very fond of this boy; but I do not think it was the fear of grieving her that made me, rather than denounce Moktir, invent some story or other to explain the loss of her scissors.

From that day onwards, Moktir became my favourite.

5

OUR stay at Biskra was not to last much longer. When the February rains were over, the outburst of heat that succeeded them was too violent. After several days of drenching downpour, one morning, suddenly, I woke in an atmosphere of brilliant blue. As soon as I was up, I hurried to the highest part of the terrace. The sky, from one horizon to the other, was cloudless. Mists were rising under the heat of the sun, which was already fierce; the whole oasis was smoking; in the distance could be heard the grumbling of the Oued in flood. The air was so pure and so delicious that I felt better at once. Marceline joined me; we wanted to go out but that day the mud kept us at home.

A few days later, we went back to Lassif's orchard; the stems of the plants looked heavy, sodden, and swollen with water. This African land, whose thirsty season of waiting was not then known to me, had lain submerged for many long days and was now awaking from its winter sleep, drunken with water, bursting with the fresh rise of sap; throughout it rang the wild laughter of an exultant spring which found an echo, a double, as it were, in my own heart. Ashour and Moktir came with us at first; I still enjoyed their slight friendship, which cost me only half a franc a day; but I soon grew tired of them; not now so weak as to need the example of their health, and no longer finding in their play the food necessary to keep my joy alive, I turned the elation of my mind and senses to Marceline. Her gladness made me realize she had been unhappy before. I excused myself like a child for having so often left her to herself, set down my odd, elusive behaviour to the score of weakness, and declared that hitherto loving had been too much for me, but that henceforward, as my health grew, so would my love. I spoke truly, but no doubt I was still very weak, for it was not till more than a month later that I desired Marceline.

In the meantime, it was getting hotter every day. There was nothing to keep us at Biskra – except the charm which afterwards called me back there. Our determination to leave was taken suddenly. In three hours our things were packed. The train started next morning at daybreak.

I remember that last night. The moon was nearly full; it streamed into my room by the wide-open window. Marceline was, I think, asleep. I had gone to bed but could not sleep. I felt myself burning with a kind of happy fever – the fever of life itself . . . I got up, dipped my hands and face in water, then, pushing open the glass doors, went out.

It was already late; not a sound; not a breath; the air itself seemed asleep. The Arab dogs, which yelp all night like jackals, could only just be heard in the distance. Facing me lay the little courtyard; the wall opposite cast a slanting band of shadow across it; the regular palm-trees, bereft of colour and life, seemed struck for ever motionless . . . But in sleep there is still some palpitation of life; here, nothing seemed asleep; everything seemed dead. The calm appalled me; and suddenly there rose in me afresh the tragic realization of my life; it came upon me as though to protest, to assert itself, to bewail itself in the silence, so violent, so impetuous, so agonizing almost, that I should have

47

cried aloud, if I could have cried like an animal. I took
hold of my hand, I remember – my left hand in my
right; I wanted to lift it to my head and I did. What
for? To assure myself that I was alive and that I felt the
wonder of it. I touched my forehead, my eyelids. Then
a shudder seized me. A day will come, thought I, a day
will come when I shall not even be strong enough to
lift to my lips the very water I most thirst for ... I
went in, but did not lie down again at once; I wanted
to fix that night, to engrave its memory on my mind, to
hold and to keep it; undecided as to what I should do, I
took a book from my table – it was the Bible – and
opened it at random; by stooping over it in the moon-
light, I could see to read; I read Christ's words to Peter
– those words, alas, which I was never to forget:
'When thou wast young, thou girdest thyself and
walkedst whither thou wouldest: but when thou shalt
be old, thou shalt stretch forth thy hands ...' – thou
shalt stretch forth thy hands ...

The next morning at dawn, we left.

6

I SHALL not speak of every stage of the journey. Some of them have left me only a confused recollection; I was sometimes better and sometimes worse in health, still at the mercy of a cold wind and made anxious by the shadow of a cloud; the condition of my nerves too was the cause of frequent trouble; but my lungs at any rate were recovering. Each relapse was shorter and less serious; the attacks were as sharp, but my body was better armed against them.

From Tunis we went to Malta, and from there to Syracuse; I found myself back again on the classic ground whose language and history were known to me. Since the beginning of my illness I had lived without question or rule, simply applying myself to the act of living as an animal does or a child. Now that I was less absorbed by my malady, my life became once more certain of itself and conscious. After that long and almost mortal sickness, I had thought I should rise again the same as before and be able without difficulty to re-knit my present to my past; in the newness of a strange country it had been possible to deceive myself – but not here; everything brought home to me – though I still thought it astonishing – that I was changed.

When at Syracuse and later, I wanted to start my work again and immerse myself once more in a minute study of the past, I discovered that something had, if not destroyed, at any rate modified my pleasure in it ... and this something was the feeling of the present. The history of the past had now taken on for me the immobility, the terrifying fixity of the nocturnal shadows in the little courtyard of Biskra – the immobility of death. In old days, I had taken pleasure in this very fixity, which enabled my mind to work with precision; the facts of history all appeared to me like specimens in a museum, or rather like plants in a herbarium, permanently dried, so that it was easy to forget they had once upon a time been juicy with sap and alive in the sun. Nowadays, if I still took any pleasure in history, it was by imagining it in the present. Thus the great political events of the past moved me less than the feeling that began to revive in me for the poets or for a few men of action. At Syracuse, I reread Theocritus and reflected that his goatherds with the beautiful names were the very same as those I had loved at Biskra.

My erudition, which was aroused at every step, became an encumbrance and hampered my joy. I could not see a Greek theatre or temple without immediately reconstructing it in my mind. Every thought of the festivals of antiquity made me grieve over the death of the ruin that was left standing in their place; and I had a horror of death.

I ended by avoiding ruins; the noblest monuments of the past were less to me than those sunk gardens of the Latomie whose lemons have the sharp sweetness of oranges – or the shores of the Cyane, still flowing among the papyri as blue as on the day when it wept for Proserpine.

I ended by despising the learning that had at first been my pride; the studies that up to then had been my whole life now seemed to me to have a mere accidental and conventional connexion with myself. I found out that I was something different and – oh rapture! – that I had a separate existence of my own. Inasmuch as I was a specialist, I appeared to myself senseless; inasmuch as I was a man, did I know myself at all? I had only just been born and could not as yet know *what* I had been born. It was that I had to find out.

There is nothing more tragic for a man who has been expecting to die than a long convalescence. After that touch from the wing of Death, what seemed important is so no longer; other things become so which had at first seemed unimportant, or which one did not even know existed. The miscellaneous mass of acquired knowledge of every kind that has overlain the mind gets peeled off in places like a mask of paint, exposing the bare skin – the very flesh of the authentic creature that had lain hidden beneath it.

He it was whom I thenceforward set out to discover – that authentic creature, 'the old Adam', whom the Gospel had repudiated, whom everything about me – books, masters, parents, and I myself had begun by attempting to suppress. And he was already coming into view, still in the rough and difficult of discovery, thanks to all that overlay him, but so much the more worthy to be discovered, so much the more valorous. Thenceforward I despised the secondary creature, the creature who was due to teaching, whom education had painted on the surface. These overlays had to be shaken off.

And I compared myself to a palimpsest; I tasted the scholar's joy when he discovers under more recent writing, and on the same paper, a very ancient and infinitely more precious text. What was this occult text? In order to read it, was it not first of all necessary to efface the more recent one?

I was besides no longer the sickly, studious being to whom my early morality, with all its rigidity and restrictions, had been suited. There was more here than a convalescence; there was an increase, a recrudescence of life, the influx of a richer, warmer blood which must of necessity affect my thoughts, touch them one by one, inform them all, stir and colour the most remote, delicate and secret fibres of my being. For, either to strength or to weakness, the creature adapts itself; it constitutes itself according to the powers it possesses; but if these should increase, if they should permit a wider scope, then . . . I did not think all this at the time, and my description gives a false idea of me. In reality, I did not think at all; I never questioned myself; a happy fatalism guided me. I was afraid that too hasty an investigation might disturb the mystery of my slow transformation. I must allow time for the effaced characters to reappear, and not attempt to re-form them. Not so much neglecting my mind therefore, as allowing it to lie fallow, I gave myself up to the luxurious enjoyment of my own self, of external things, of all existence, which seemed to me divine. We had left Syracuse, and as I ran along the precipitous road that connects Taormina with Mola, I remember shouting aloud, as if my calling could bring him to me: 'A new self! A new self!'

My only effort then – an effort which was at that time constant – consisted in systematically condemning and suppressing everything which I believed I owed to my past education and early moral beliefs. Deliberately disdainful of my learning, and in scorn of my scholar's tastes, I refused to visit Agrigentum, and a few days later, on the road to Naples, I passed by the beautiful temple of Paestum, in which Greece still breathes, and where, two years later, I went to worship some God or other – I no longer know which.

Why do I say 'my only effort'? How could I be interested in myself save as a perfectible being? Never before had my will been so tensely strung as in striving after this unknown and vaguely imagined perfection. I employed the whole of my will indeed, in strengthening and bronzing my body. We had left the coast near Salerno and reached Ravello. There, a keener air, the charm of the rocks, their recesses, their surprises, the unexplored depths of the valleys, all contributed to my strength and enjoyment and gave impetus to my enthusiasm.

Not far from the shore and very near the sky, Ravello lies on an abrupt height facing the flat and distant coast of Paestum. Under the Norman domination, it was a city of no inconsiderable importance; it is nothing now but a narrow village where I think we were the only strangers. We were lodged in an ancient religious house which had been turned into a hotel; it is situated on the extreme edge of the rock, and its terraces and gardens seemed to hang suspended over an abyss of azure. Over the wall, festooned with creeping vine, one could at first see nothing but the sea; one had to go right up to the wall in order to discover the steep cultivated slope that connects Ravello with the shore by paths that seem more like staircases. Above Ravello, the mountain continues. First come enormous olive and caroub trees, with cyclamen growing in their shadow; then, higher up, Spanish chestnuts in great quantities, cool air, northern plants; lower down lemon trees near the sea. These are planted in small plots owing to the slope of the ground; they are step gardens, nearly all alike; a narrow path goes from end to end through the middle of each; one enters noiselessly, like a thief; one dreams in their green shadow; their foliage is thick and heavy; no direct ray of sunlight penetrates it; the lemons, like drops of opaque wax, hang perfumed; they are white and greenish in the shade; they are within reach of one's hand, of one's thirst; they are sweet and sharp and refreshing.

The shade was so dense beneath them that I did not dare linger in it after my walk, for exercise still made me perspire. And yet I now managed the steps without being exhausted; I practised climbing them with my mouth shut; I put greater and greater intervals between my halts; 'I will go so far without giving in,' I used to say to myself; then, the goal reached, I was rewarded by a glow of satisfied pride; I would take a few long deep breaths, and feel as if the air entered my lungs more thoroughly, more efficaciously. I brought all my old assiduity to bear on the care of my body. I began to progress.

I was sometimes astonished that my health came back so quickly. I began to think I had exaggerated the gravity of my condition – to doubt that I had been very ill – to laugh at my blood-spitting – to regret that my recovery had not been more arduous.

In my ignorance of my physical needs, my treatment of myself had at first been very foolish. I now made a patient study of them and came to regard my ingenious exercise of prudence and care as a kind of game. What I still suffered from most was my morbid sensitiveness to the slightest change of temperature. Now that my lungs were cured, I attributed this hyperaesthesia to the nervous debility left me by my illness and I determined to conquer it. The sight of the beautiful, brown, sunburned skins which some of the carelessly clad peasants at work in the fields showed beneath their open shirts, made me long to be like them. One morning, after I had stripped, I looked at myself; my thin arms, my stooping shoulders, which no effort of mine could keep straight, but above all the whiteness of my skin, or rather its entire want of colour, shamed me to tears. I dressed quickly and, instead of going down to Amalfi as usual, I turned my steps towards some mossy, grass-grown rocks, in a place far from any habitation, far from any road, where I knew no one could see me. When I got there, I undressed slowly. The air was almost sharp, but the sun was burning. I exposed my whole body to its flame. I sat down, lay down, turned myself about. I felt the ground hard beneath me; the waving grass brushed me. Though I was sheltered from the wind, I shivered and thrilled at every breath. Soon a delicious burning enveloped me; my whole being surged up into my skin.

We stayed at Ravello a fortnight; every morning I returned to the same rocks and went on with my cure. I soon found I was wearing a troublesome and unnecessary amount of clothing; my skin having recovered its tone, the constant perspiration ceased and I was able to keep warm without superfluous protection.

On one of the last mornings (we were in the middle of April), I was bolder still. In a hollow of the rocks I have mentioned, there flowed a spring of transparent water. At this very place it fell in a little cascade – not a very abundant one to be sure, but the fall had hollowed out a deeper basin at its foot in which the water lingered, exquisitely pure and clear. Three times already I had been there, leaned over it, stretched myself along its bank, thirsty and longing; I had gazed at the bottom of polished rock, where not a stain, not a weed was to be seen, and where the sun shot its dancing and iridescent rays. On this fourth day, I came to the spot with my mind already made up. The water looked as bright and as clear as ever, and without pausing to think, I plunged straight in. It struck an instant chill through me and I jumped out again quickly and flung myself down on the grass in the sun. There was some wild thyme growing near by; I picked some of the sweet-smelling leaves, crushed them in my hands, and rubbed my wet but burning body with them. I looked at myself for a long while – with no more shame now – with joy. Although not yet robust, I felt myself capable of becoming so – harmonious, sensuous, almost beautiful.

7

AND so, in the place of all action and all work, I contented myself with physical exercises, which certainly implied a change in my moral outlook, but which I soon began to regard as mere training, as simply a means to an end, and no longer satisfying in themselves.

I will tell you, however, about one other action of mine, though perhaps you will consider it ridiculous, for its very childishness marks the need that then tormented me of showing by some outward sign the change that had come over my inward self: at Amalfi I had my beard and moustache shaved off. Up till that day I had worn them long and my hair cropped close. It had never occurred to me that I could do anything else. And suddenly, on the day when I first stripped myself on the rock, my beard made me feel uncomfortable; it was like a last piece of clothing I could not get rid of; I felt as if it were false; it was carefully cut – not in a point, but square, and it then and there struck me as very ugly and ridiculous. When I got back to my hotel room, I looked at myself in the glass and was displeased with my appearance; I looked like what I had hitherto been – an archaeologist – a bookworm. Immediately after lunch, I went down to Amalfi with my mind made up. The town is very small and I could find nothing better than a vulgar little shop in the piazza. It was market day; the place was full; I had to wait interminably; but nothing – neither the suspicious-looking razors, nor the dirty yellow shaving-brush, nor the smell, nor the barber's talk could put me off. When my beard fell beneath his scissors, I felt as though I had taken off a mask. But oh! when I saw myself, the emotion that filled me and which I tried to keep down, was not pleasure, but fear. I do not criticize this feeling – I record it. I thought myself quite good-looking ... no, the reason of my fear was a feeling that my mind had been stripped of all disguise, and it suddenly appeared to me redoubtable.

On the other hand, I let my hair grow.

That is all my new and still unoccupied self found to do. I expected it eventually to give birth to actions that would astonish me – but later – later, I said to myself, when it is more fully formed. In the meantime, as I was obliged to live, I was reduced, like Descartes, to a provisional mode of action. This was the reason Marceline did not notice anything. The different look in my eyes, no doubt, and the changed expression of my features, especially on the day when I appeared without any beard, might perhaps have aroused her suspicions, but she already loved me too much to see me as I was; and then I did my best to reassure her. The important thing was that she should not interfere with my renascent life, and to keep it from her eyes, I had to dissemble.

For that matter, the man Marceline loved, the man she had married, was not my 'new self'. So I told myself again and again as an excuse for hiding him. In this way I showed her an image of myself, which by the very fact of its remaining constant and faithful to the past, became every day falser and falser.

For the time being, therefore, my relationship with Marceline remained the same, though it was every day getting more intense by reason of my growing love. My dissimulation (if that expression can be applied to the need I felt of protecting my thoughts from her judgement), my very dissimulation increased that love. I mean that it kept me incessantly occupied with Marceline. At first, perhaps, this necessity for falsehood cost me a little effort; but I soon came to understand that the things that are reputed worst (lying, to mention only one) are only difficult to do as long as one has never done them; but that they become – and very quickly too – easy, pleasant, and agreeable to do over again, and soon even natural. So then, as is always the case when one overcomes an initial disgust, I ended by taking pleasure in my dissimulation itself, by protracting it, as if it afforded opportunity for the play of my undiscovered faculties. And every day my life grew richer and fuller, as I advanced towards a riper, more delicious happiness.

8

THE road from Ravello to Sorrento is so beautiful that I had no desire that morning to see anything more beautiful on earth. The sun-warmed harshness of the rocks, the air's abundance, the scents, the limpidity, all filled me with the heavenly delight of living, and with such contentment that there seemed to dwell in me nothing but a dancing joy; memories and regrets, hope and desire, future and past were alike silent; I was conscious of nothing in life but what the moment brought, but what the moment carried away.

'O joys of the body!' I exclaimed; 'unerring rhythm of the muscles! health! ...'

I had started early that morning, ahead of Marceline, for her calmer pleasure would have cooled mine, just as her slower pace would have kept me back. She was to join me by carriage at Positano, where we were to lunch.

I was nearing Positano, when a noise of wheels, which sounded like the bass accompaniment to a curious kind of singing, made me look round abruptly. At first I could see nothing because of a turn in the road, which in that place follows the edge of the cliff; then a carriage driven at a frantic pace dashed suddenly into view; it was Marceline's. The driver was singing at the top of his voice, standing up on the box and gesticulating violently, while he ferociously whipped his frightened horse. What a brute the fellow was! He passed me so quickly that I only just had time to get out of the way and my shouts failed to make him stop

... I rushed after him, but the carriage was going too fast. I was terrified that Marceline would fling herself out of the carriage, and equally so that she would stay in it; a single jolt might have thrown her into the sea ... All of a sudden the horse fell down. Marceline jumped out and started running, but I was beside her in a moment ... The driver, as soon as he saw me, broke into horrible oaths. I was furious with the man; at his first word of abuse, I rushed at him and flung him brutally from his box. I rolled on the ground with him, but did not lose my advantage; he seemed dazed by his fall and was soon still more so by a blow on the face which I gave him, when I saw he meant to bite me. I did not let go of him, however, and pressed with my knee on his chest, while I tried to pinion his arms. I looked at his ugly face, which my fist had made still uglier; he spat, foamed, bled, swore; oh, what a horrible creature! He deserved strangling, I thought. And perhaps I should have strangled him – at any rate, I felt capable of it; and I really believe it was only the thought of the police that prevented me.

I succeeded, not without difficulty, in tying the madman up, and flung him into the carriage like a sack.

Ah! what looks, what kisses Marceline and I exchanged when it was all over. The danger had not been great; but I had had to show my strength, and that in order to protect her. At the moment I felt I could have given my life for her ... and given it wholly with joy ... The horse got up. We left the drunkard at the bottom of the carriage, got on to the box together, and drove as best we could, first to Positano, and then to Sorrento.

It was that night that I first possessed Marceline.

Have you really understood or must I tell you again that I was as it were new to things of love? Perhaps it was to its novelty that our wedding night owed its grace ... For it seems to me, when I recall it, that that first night of ours was our only one, the expectation and the surprise of love added so much deliciousness to its pleasures – so sufficient is a single night for the expression of the greatest love, and so obstinately does my memory recall that night alone. It was a flashing moment that caught and mingled our souls in its laughter ... But I believe there comes a point in love, once and no more, which later on the soul seeks – yes, seeks in vain – to surpass; I believe that happiness wears out in the effort made to recapture it; that nothing is more fatal to happiness than the remembrance of happiness. Alas! I remember that night ...

Our hotel was outside the town and surrounded with gardens and orchards; a very large balcony opened out from our room and the branches of the trees brushed against it. Our wide-open windows let in the dawn freely. I got up and bent tenderly over Marceline. She was asleep; she looked as though she were smiling in her sleep; my greater strength seemed to make me feel her greater delicacy and that her grace was all fragility. Tumultuous thoughts whirled in my brain. I reflected that she was telling the truth when she said I was her all; then, 'What do I do for her happiness?' I thought. 'Almost all day and every day I abandon her; her every hope is in me and I neglect her! ... oh, poor, poor Marceline!' My eyes filled with tears. I tried in vain to seek an excuse in my past weakness; what need had I now for so much care and attention, for so much egoism? Was I not now the stronger of the two?

The smile had left her cheeks; daybreak, though it had touched everything else with gold, suddenly showed her to me sad and pale; and perhaps the approach of morning inclined me to be anxious. 'Shall I in my turn have to nurse you, fear for you, Marceline?' I inwardly cried. I shuddered, and, overflowing with love, pity, and tenderness, I placed between her closed eyes the gentlest, the most lover-like, the most pious of kisses.

THE few days we stayed at Sorrento were smiling days and very calm. Had I ever enjoyed before such rest, such happiness? Should I ever enjoy them again? ... I spent almost all my time with Marceline; thinking less of myself, I was able to think more of her, and now took as much pleasure in talking to her as I had before taken in being silent.

I was at first astonished to feel that she looked upon our wandering life, with which I professed myself perfectly satisfied, only as something temporary; but its idleness soon became obvious to me; I agreed it must not last; for the first time, thanks to the leisure left me by my recovered health, there awoke in me a desire for work, and I began to speak seriously of going home; from Marceline's joy, I realized she herself had long been thinking of it.

Meanwhile, when I again began to turn my attention to some of my old historical studies, I found that I no longer took the same pleasure in them. As I have already told you, since my illness I had come to consider this abstract and neutral acquaintance with the past as mere vanity. In other days I had worked at philological research, studying more especially, for instance, the influence of the Goths on the corruption of the Latin language, and had passed over and misunderstood the figures of Theodoric, Cassiodorus, and Amalasontha, and their admirable and astonishing passions, in order to concentrate all my enthusiasm on mere signs – the waste product of their lives.

At present, however, these same signs, and indeed philology as a whole, were nothing more to me than a means of penetrating farther into things whose savage grandeur and nobility had begun to dawn on me. I resolved to study this period further, to limit myself for a time to the last years of the empire of the Goths, and to turn to account our coming stay at Ravenna, the scene of its closing agonies.

But shall I confess that the figure of the young king Athalaric was what attracted me most? I pictured to myself this fifteen-year-old boy, worked on in secret by the Goths, in revolt against his mother Amalasontha, rebelling against his Latin education and flinging aside his culture, as a restive horse shakes off a troublesome harness; I saw him preferring the society of the un-tutored Goths to that of Cassiodorus – too old and too wise – plunging for a few years into a life of violent and unbridled pleasures with rude companions of his own age, and dying at eighteen, rotten and sodden with debauchery. I recognized in this tragic impulse towards a wilder, more natural state, something of what Marceline used to call my 'crisis'. I tried to find some satisfaction in applying my mind to it, since it no longer occupied my body; and in Athalaric's horrible death, I did my best to read a lesson.

So we settled to spend a fortnight at Ravenna, visit Rome and Florence rapidly, then, giving up Venice and Verona, hurry over the end of our journey and not stop again before reaching Paris. I found a pleasure I had never felt before in talking to Marceline about the future; we were still a little undecided as to how we should spend the summer; we were both tired of travelling and I was in need of absolute quiet for my work; then we thought of a place of mine, situated between Lisieux and Pont-L'Évêque, in the greenest of green Normandy; it had formerly belonged to my mother, and I had passed several summers there with her in my childhood, though I had never gone back to it since her death. My father had left it in charge of a bailiff, an old man by now, who collected the rents and sent them to us regularly. I had kept enchanting memories of a large and very pleasant house standing in a garden watered by running streams; it was called La Morinière; I thought it would be good to live there.

I spoke of spending the following winter in Rome, but as a worker this time, not a tourist ... But this last plan was soon upset. Amongst the number of letters we found waiting for us at Naples was one containing an unexpected piece of information – a chair at the Collège de France had fallen vacant and my name had been several times mentioned in connexion with it; it was only a temporary post which would leave me free in the future; the friend who wrote advised me of the few steps to be taken in case I should accept, which he strongly advised me to do. I hesitated to bind myself to what at first seemed to me slavery; but then I reflected that it might be interesting to put forward my ideas on Cassiodorus in a course of lectures ... The pleasure I should be giving Marceline finally decided me, and my decision once taken, I saw only its advantages.

My father had several connexions in the learned world of Rome and Florence, with whom I had myself been in correspondence. They gave me every facility for making the necessary researches in Ravenna and elsewhere; I had no thoughts now but for my work. Marceline, by her constant consideration and in a thousand charming ways, did all she could to help me.

Our happiness during those last days of travel was so equable, so calm, that there is nothing to say about it. Men's finest works bear the persistent marks of pain. What would there be in a story of happiness? Only what prepares it, only what destroys it can be told. I have now told you what prepared it.

SECOND PART

I

WE arrived at La Morinière in the first days of July, having stayed in Paris only just long enough to do our shopping and pay a very few visits.

La Morinière is situated, as I have told you, between Lisieux and Pont-L'Évêque in the shadiest, wettest country I know. Innumerable narrow combes and gently rounded hills terminate near the wide Vallée d'Auge, which then stretches in an uninterrupted plain as far as the sea. There is no horizon; some few copse-woods, filled with mysterious shade, some few fields of corn, but chiefly meadow land – softly sloping pastures, where the lush grass is mown twice a year, where the apple-trees, when the sun is low, join shadow to shadow, where flocks and herds graze untended; in every hollow there is water – pond or pool or river; from every side comes the continual murmur of streams.

Oh, how well I remember the house! its blue roofs, its walls of stone and brick, its moat, the reflections in the still waters ... It was an old house which would easily have lodged a dozen persons; Marceline, three servants, and myself, who occasionally lent a helping hand, found it all we could do to animate a part of it. Our old bailiff, who was called Bocage, had already done his best to prepare some of the rooms; the old furniture awoke from its twenty years' slumber; everything had remained just as I remembered it – the panelling not too dilapidated, the rooms easy to live in.

Bocage, to welcome us, had put flowers in all the vases he could lay hands on. He had had the large courtyard and the nearest paths in the park weeded and raked. When we arrived, the sun's last rays were falling on the house, and from the valley facing it a mist had arisen which hovered there motionless, masking and revealing the river. We had not well arrived, when all at once I recognized the scent of the grass; and when I heard the piercing cries of the swallows as they flew round the house, the whole past suddenly rose up, as though it had been lying in wait for my approach to close over and submerge me.

In a few days the house was more or less comfortable; I might have settled down to work; but I delayed, at first still listening to the voice of my past as it recalled its slightest details to my memory, and then too much absorbed by an unwonted emotion. Marceline, a week after our arrival, confided to me that she was expecting a child.

Thenceforward I thought I owed her redoubled care, and that she had a right to greater tenderness than ever; at any rate during the first weeks that followed her confidence, I spent almost every minute of the day in her company. We used to go and sit near the wood, on a bench where in old days I had been used to sit with my mother; there, each moment brought us a richer pleasure, each hour passed with a smoother flow. If no distinct memory of this period of my life stands out for me, it is not because I am less deeply grateful for it – but because everything in it melted and mingled into a state of changeless ease, in which evening joined morning without a break, in which day passed into day without a surprise.

70

I gradually set to work again with a quiet mind in possession of itself, certain of its strength, looking calmly and confidently to the future; with a will that seemed softened, as though by hearkening to the counsels of that temperate land.

There can be no doubt, I thought, that the example of such a land, where everything is ripening towards fruition and harvest, must have the best of influences on me. I looked forward with admiring wonder to the tranquil promise of the great oxen and fat cows that grazed in those opulent meadows. The apple-trees, planted in order on the sunniest slopes of the hillsides, gave hopes this summer of a magnificent crop. I saw in my mind's eye the rich burden of fruit which would soon bow down their branches. From this ordered abundance, this joyous acceptance of service imposed, the smiling cultivation, had arisen a harmony that was the result not of chance but of intention, a rhythm, a beauty, at once human and natural, in which the teeming fecundity of nature and the wise effort of man to regulate it were combined in such perfect agreement that one no longer knew which was more admirable. What would man's effort be worth, thought I, without the savagery of the power it controls? What would the wild rush of these upwelling forces become without the intelligent effort that banks it, curbs it, leads it by such pleasant ways to its outcome of luxury? And I let myself go in a dream of lands where every force should be so regulated, all expenditure so compensated, all exchanges so strict, that the slightest waste would be appreciable; then I applied my dream to life and imagined a code of ethics which should institute the scientific and perfect utilization of a man's self by a controlling intelligence.

Where had my rebelliousness vanished to? Where was it hiding itself? It seemed never to have existed, so tranquil was I. The rising tide of my love had swept it all away.

Meanwhile old Bocage bustled round us; he gave directions, he superintended, he advised; his need of feeling himself indispensable was tiresome in the extreme. In order not to hurt his feelings I had to go over his accounts and listen for hours to his endless explanations. Even that was not enough; I had to visit the estate with him. His sententious truisms, his continual speeches, his evident self-satisfaction, the display he made of his honesty drove me to exasperation; he became more and more persistent and there was nothing I would not have done to recover my liberty, when an unexpected occurrence brought about a change in my relations with him. One evening Bocage announced that he was expecting his son Charles the next day.

I said, 'Oh!' rather casually, having so far troubled myself very little as to any children Bocage might or might not have; then, seeing that my indifference offended him and that he expected some expression of interest and surprise, 'Where has he been?' I asked.

'In a model farm near Alençon,' answered Bocage.

'How old is he now? About . . .?' I went on, calculating the age of this son, of whose existence I had so far been totally unaware, and leaving him time enough to interrupt me . . .

'Past seventeen,' went on Bocage. 'He was not much more than four when your father's good lady died. Ah! He's a big lad now; he'll know more than his dad soon . . . ' Once Bocage was started, nothing could stop him, not even the boredom I very plainly showed.

I had forgotten all about this, when the next evening, Charles, newly arrived from his journey, came to pay his respects to Marceline and me. He was a fine strong young fellow, so exuberantly healthy, so lissom, so well-made, that not even the frightful town clothes he had put on in our honour could make him look ridiculous; his shyness hardly added anything to the fine natural red of his cheeks. He did not look more than fifteen, his eyes were so bright and so childlike; he expressed himself clearly, without embarrassment, and, unlike his father, did not speak when he had nothing to say. I cannot remember what we talked about that first evening; I was so busy looking at him that I found nothing to say and let Marceline do all the talking. But next day, for the first time, I did not wait for old Bocage to come and fetch me, in order to go down to the farm, where I knew they were starting work on a pond that had to be repaired.

This pond – almost as big as a lake – was leaking. The leak had been located and had to be cemented. In order to do this, the pond had first to be drained, a thing that had not been done for fifteen years. It was full of carp and tench, great creatures, some of them, that lay at the bottom of the pond without ever coming up. I wanted to stock the moat with some of these fish and give some to the labourers, so that upon this occasion the pleasure of a fishing party was added to the day's work as could be seen from the extraordinary animation of the farm; some children from the neighbourhood had joined the workers and Marceline herself had promised to come down later.

The water had already been sinking for some time when I got there. Every now and then a great ripple suddenly stirred its surface and the brown backs of the disturbed fish came into sight. The children paddling in the puddles round the edges amused themselves with catching gleaming handfuls of small fry, which they flung into pails of clear water. The water in the pond was muddy and soon became more and more thick and troubled owing to the agitation of the fish. Their abundance was beyond all expectation: four farm labourers, dipping into the water at random, pulled them out in handfuls. I was sorry that Marceline had not arrived and decided to run and fetch her, when a shout signalled the appearance of the first eels. But no one could succeed in catching them; they slipped between the men's fingers. Charles, who up till then had been standing beside his father on the bank, could restrain himself no longer; he took off his shoes and socks in a moment, flung aside his coat and waistcoat, then, tucking up his trousers and shirtsleeves as high as they would go, stepped resolutely into the mud. I immediately did the same.

'Charles!' I cried, 'it was a good thing you came back yesterday, wasn't it?' He was already too busy with his fishing to answer, but he looked at me, laughing. I called him after a moment to help me catch a big eel; we joined hands in trying to hold it ... Then came another and another; our faces were splashed with mud; sometimes the ooze suddenly gave way beneath us and we sank into it up to our waists; we were soon drenched. In the ardour of the sport, we barely exchanged a shout or two, a word or two; but at the end of the day, I became aware I was saying

74

'thou' to Charles, without having any clear idea when I had begun. Our work in common had taught us more about each other than a long conversation. Marceline had not come yet; she did not come at all, but I ceased to regret her absence; I felt as though she would have a little spoiled our pleasure.

Early next morning, I went down to the farm to look for Charles. We took our way together to the woods.

As I myself knew very little about my estate and was not much distressed at knowing so little, I was astonished to find how much Charles knew about it and about the way it was farmed; he told me what I was barely aware of, namely, that I had six farmer-tenants, that the rents might have amounted to sixteen or eighteen thousand francs, and that if they actually amounted to barely half that sum, it was because almost everything was eaten up by repairs of all sorts and by the payment of middle-men. His way of smiling as he looked at the fields in cultivation soon made me suspect that the management of the estate was not quite so good as I had at first thought and as Bocage had given me to understand; I pressed Charles further on this subject, and the intelligence of practical affairs which had so exasperated me in Bocage, amused me in a child like him. We continued our walks day after day; the estate was large and when we had visited every corner of it, we began again with more method. Charles did not hide his irritation at the sight of certain fields, certain pieces of land that were overgrown with gorse, thistles, and weeds; he instilled into me his hatred of fallow land and set me dreaming with him of a better mode of agriculture.

'But,' I said to him at first, 'who is it that suffers from

this lack of cultivation? Isn't it only the farmer himself? However much the profits of his farm vary, his rent still remains the same.'

Charles was a little annoyed: 'You understand nothing about it,' he ventured to say – and I smiled. 'You think only of income and won't consider that the capital is deteriorating. Your land is slowly losing its value by being badly cultivated.'

'If it were to bring in more by being better cultivated, I expect the farmers would set about it. They are too eager for gain not to make as much profit as they can.'

'You are not counting,' continued Charles, 'the cost of increased labour. These neglected bits of land are sometimes a long way from the farms. True, if they were cultivated, they would bring in nothing or next to nothing, but at any rate, they would keep from spoiling.'

And so the conversation went on. Sometimes for an hour on end we seemed to be interminably repeating the same things as we walked over the fields; but I listened, and little by little gathered information.

'After all, it's your father's business,' I said one day impatiently. Charles blushed a little.

'My father is old,' he said; 'he has a great deal to do already, seeing to the upkeep of the buildings, collecting the rents, and so on. It's not his business to make reforms.'

'And what reforms would *you* make?' I asked. But at that he became evasive and pretended he knew nothing about it; it was only by insisting that I forced him to explain.

'I should take away all the uncultivated fields from

the tenants,' he ended by advising. 'If the farmers leave part of their land uncultivated, it's a proof they don't need it all in order to pay you; or if they say they must keep it all, I should raise their rents. All the people hereabouts are idle,' he added.

Of the six farms that belonged to me, the one I most liked visiting was situated on a hill that overlooked La Morinière; it was called La Valterie; the farmer who rented it was a pleasant enough fellow and I used to like talking to him. Nearer La Morinière was a farm called the 'home farm', which was let on a system that left Bocage, pending the landlord's absence, in possession of part of the cattle. Now that my doubts had been awakened I began to suspect honest Bocage himself, if not of cheating me, at any rate, of allowing other people to cheat me. One stable and one cow-house were, it is true, reserved to me, but it soon dawned upon me that they had merely been invented so as to allow the farmer to feed his cows and horses with my oats and hay. So far, I had listened indulgently to the very unconvincing reports which Bocage gave me from time to time of deaths, malformations, and diseases. I swallowed everything. It had not then occurred to me that it was sufficient for one of the farmer's cows to fall ill for it to become one of my cows, nor that it was sufficient for one of my cows to do well for it to become one of the farmer's; but a few rash remarks of Charles's, a few observations of my own began to enlighten me, and my mind, once given the hint, worked quickly.

Marceline, at my suggestion, went over the accounts minutely, but could find nothing wrong with them; Bocage's honesty was displayed on every page. What was to be done? Let things be. At any rate, I now watched the management of the cattle in a state of suppressed indignation, but without letting it be too obvious.

I had four horses and ten cows – quite enough to be a considerable worry to me. Among my four horses was one which was still called 'the colt', though it was more than three years old; it was now being broken in. I was beginning to take an interest in it, when one fine morning I was informed that it was perfectly un-manageable, that it would be impossible ever to do anything with it and that the best thing would be to get rid of it. As if on purpose to convince me of this, in case I had doubted it, it had been made to break the front of a small cart and had cut its hocks in doing so.

I had much ado that day to keep my temper, but what helped me was Bocage's obvious embarrassment. After all, thought I, he is more weak than anything else; it is the men who are to blame, but they want a guiding hand over them.

I went into the yard to see the colt; one of the men who had been beating it began to stroke it as soon as he heard me coming; I pretended to have seen nothing. I did not know much about horses, but this colt seemed to me a fine animal; it was half-bred, light bay in colour and remarkably elegant in shape, with a very bright eye and a very light mane and tail. I made sure it had not been injured, insisted on its cuts being properly dressed, and went away without another word.

That evening, as soon as I saw Charles, I tried to find out what he personally thought of the colt.

'I think he's a perfectly quiet beast,' he said, 'but

they don't know how to manage him; they'll drive him wild.'

'And how would *you* manage him?'

'Will you let me have him for a week, Sir? I'll answer for him.'

'And what will you do?'

'You will see.'

The next morning, Charles took the colt down to a corner of the field that was shaded by a superb walnut-tree and bordered by the river; I went too, together with Marceline. It is one of my most vivid recollections. Charles had tied the colt with a rope a few yards long to a stake firmly planted in the ground. The mettlesome creature had, it seems, objected for some time with great spirit; but now, tired and quieted, it was going round more calmly; the elasticity of its trot was astonishing and as delightful and engaging to watch as a dance. Charles stood in the centre of the circle and avoided the rope at every round with a sudden leap, exciting or calming the beast with his voice; he held a long whip in his hand, but I did not see him use it. Everything about his look and move-ments – his youthfulness, his delight – gave his work the fervent and beautiful aspect of pleasure. Suddenly – I have no idea how – he was astride the animal; it had slackened its pace and then stopped; he had patted it a little and then, all of a sudden I saw that he was on its back, sure of himself, barely holding its mane, laugh-ing, leaning forward, still patting and stroking its neck. The colt had hardly resisted for a moment; then it began its even trot again, so handsome, so easy, that I envied Charles and told him so.

'A few days' more training and the saddle won't

tickle him at all; in a fortnight, Sir, your lady herself won't be afraid to mount him; he'll be as quiet as a lamb.'

It was quite true; a few days later, the horse allowed himself to be stroked, harnessed, led, without any signs of restiveness; and Marceline might really have ridden him if her state of health had permitted.

'You ought to try him yourself, Sir,' said Charles.

I should never have done so alone; but Charles suggested saddling another of the farm horses for himself, and the pleasure of accompanying him proved irresistible.

How grateful I was to my mother for having sent me to a riding-school when I was a boy! The recollection of those long-ago lessons stood me in good stead. The sensation of feeling myself on horseback was not too strange; after the first few moments, I had no tremors and felt perfectly at ease. Charles's mount was heavier; it was not pure bred, but far from bad-looking, and above all, Charles rode it well. We got into the habit of going out every day; for choice, we started in the early morning, through grass that was still bright with dew; we rode to the limit of the woods; the dripping hazels, shaken by our passage, drenched us with their showers; suddenly the horizon opened out; there, in front of us, lay the vast Vallée d'Auge and far in the distance could be divined the presence of the sea. We stayed a moment without dismounting; the rising sun coloured the mists, parted them, dispersed them; then we set off again at a brisk trot; we lingered a little at the farm, where the work was only just beginning; we enjoyed for a moment the proud pleasure of being earlier than the labourers – of looking down on them; then,

abruptly, we left them; I was home again at La Morinière just as Marceline was beginning to get up.

I used to come in drunk with the open air, dazed with
speed, my limbs a little stiff with a delicious fatigue, all
health and appetite and freshness. Marceline approved,
encouraged my fancy. I went straight to her room, still
in my gaiters, and found her lingering in bed, waiting
for me; I came bringing with me a scent of wet leaves,
which she said she liked. And she listened while I told
her of our ride, of the awakening of the fields, of the
recommencing of the day's labour . . . She took as much
delight, it seemed, in feeling me live as in living herself.
Soon I trespassed on this delight too; our rides grew
longer, and sometimes I did not come in till nearly
noon.

I kept the afternoons and evenings, however, as
much as possible for the preparation of my lectures.
My work on them made good progress; I was satisfied
with it and thought they might perhaps be worth pub-
lishing later as a book. By a kind of natural reaction,
the more regular and orderly my life became and the
more pleasure I took in establishing order about me –
the more attracted I felt by the rude ethics of the Goths.
With a boldness for which I was afterwards blamed, I
took the line throughout my lectures of making the
apology and eulogy of nonculture; but, at the same
time, in my private life, I was laboriously doing all I
could to control, if not to suppress, everything about
me and within me that in any way suggested it. How
far did I not push this wisdom – or this folly?

Two of my tenants whose leases expired at Christmas
time came to me with a request for renewal; it was a
matter of signing the usual preliminary agreement.

Strong in Charles's assurances and encouraged by his daily conversations, I awaited the farmers with resolution. They on the other hand, equally strong in the conviction that tenants are hard to replace, began by asking for their rents to be lowered. Their stupefaction was great when I read them the agreement I had myself drawn up, in which I not only refused to lower the rents but also withdrew from the farms certain portions of land, which I said they were making no use of. They pretended at first to take it as a laughing matter – I must be joking. What could I do with the land? It was worth nothing; and if they made no use of it, it was because no use could be made of it . . . Then, seeing I was serious, they turned obstinate; I was obstinate too. They thought they would frighten me by threatening to leave. It was what I was waiting for:

'All right! Go if you like! I won't keep you,' I said, tearing the agreement up before their eyes.

So there I was, with more than two hundred acres left on my hands. I had planned for some time past to give the chief management of this land to Bocage, thinking that in this way I should be giving it indirectly to Charles; my intention also was to look after it a good deal myself; but in reality, I reflected very little about it; the very risk of the undertaking tempted me. The tenants would not be turning out before Christmas; between this and then we should have time to look about us. I told Charles; his delight annoyed me; he could not hide it; it made me feel more than ever that he was much too young. We were already pressed for time; it was the season when the reaping of the crops leaves the fields empty for early ploughing. By an established custom, the outgoing tenant works side by side with the incoming; the former quits the land bit by bit, as soon as he has carried his crops. I was afraid the two farmers I had dismissed would somehow revenge themselves on me; but, on the contrary, they made a pretence of being perfectly amiable (I only learned later how much they benefited by this). I took advantage of their complaisance to go up to their land – which was soon going to be mine – every morning and evening. Autumn was beginning; more labourers had to be hired to get on with the ploughing and sowing; we had bought harrows, rollers, ploughs; I rode about on horseback, superintending and directing the work, taking pleasure in ordering people about and in using my authority.

Meanwhile, in the neighbouring meadows, the apples were being gathered; they dropped from the trees and lay rolling in the thick grass; never had there been a more abundant crop; there were not enough pickers; they had to be brought in from the neighbouring villages and taken on for a week; Charles and I sometimes amused ourselves by helping them. Some of the men beat the branches with sticks to bring down the late fruit; the fruit that fell of itself was gathered into separate heaps; often the overripe apples lay bruised and crushed in the long grass so that it was impossible to walk without stepping on them. The smell that rose from the ground was acrid and sickly and mingled with the smell of the ploughed land.

Autumn was advancing. The mornings of the last fine days are the freshest, the most limpid of all. There were times when the moisture-laden atmosphere painted all the distances blue, made them look more distant still, turned a short walk into a day's journey;

and the whole country looked bigger; at times again the abnormal transparency of the air brought the horizon closer; it seemed as though it might be reached by one stroke of the wing; and I could not tell which of the two states filled me with a heavier languor. My work was almost finished – at least, so I told myself, as an encouragement to be idle. The time I did not spend at the farm, I spent with Marceline. Together we went out into the garden; we walked slowly, she languidly hanging on my arm; the bench where we went to sit looked over the valley, which the evening gradually filled with light. She had a tender way of leaning against my shoulder; and we would stay so till evening, motionless, speechless, letting the day sink and melt within us … In what a cloak of silence our love had already learned to wrap itself! For already Marceline's love was stronger than words – for sometimes her love was almost an anguish to me. As a breath of wind sometimes ripples the surface of a tranquil pool, the slightest emotion was visible in her face; she was listening now to the new life mysteriously quivering within her, and I leaned over her as over deep transparent water where, as far as the eye could reach, nothing was to be seen but love. Ah! if this was still happiness, I know I did my best to hold it, as one tries – in vain – to hold the water that slips between one's joined hands; but already I felt, close beside my happiness, something not happiness, something indeed that coloured my love, but with the colours of autumn.

Autumn was passing. Every morning the grass was wetter, till it no longer dried in the fringe of the woods on the shady side of the valley; at the first streak of dawn, it was white. The ducks on the waters of the moat fluttered and flapped their wings; they grew fiercely agitated; sometimes they rose together, calling loudly, and flew in a noisy flight right round La Morinière. One morning we missed them. Bocage had shut them up. Charles told me that every autumn at migration time they had to be shut up in this way. And a few days later the weather changed. One evening, suddenly, there came a great blast, a breath from the sea, stormy, steady, bringing with it cold and rain, carrying off the birds of passage. Marceline's condition, the business of settling into a new apartment, the work entailed by my lectures, would in any case have soon called us back to town. The bad weather, which began early, drove us away at once.

It is true that the farm affairs were to bring me back in November. I was greatly vexed to hear of Bocage's plans for the winter; he told me that he wished to send Charles back to his model farm where, so he declared, he had still a great deal to learn; I talked to him long, used all the arguments I could think of, but I could not make him budge; at the outside, he consented to shorten Charles's training by a trifle so as to allow him to come back a little sooner. Bocage did not conceal from me that the running of the two farms would be a matter of no small difficulty; but he had in view, so he said, two highly trustworthy peasants whom he intended to employ; they would be partly farmers, partly tenants, partly labourers; the thing was too unusual in these parts for him to hope much good would come of it; but, he said, it was my own wish. This conversation took place towards the end of October. In the first days of November, we moved to Paris.

2

It was in S— Street, near Passy, that we took up our residence. The apartment, which had been found for us by one of Marceline's brothers, and which we had visited when we had last passed through Paris, was much bigger than the one my father had left me, and Marceline was a little uneasy, not only at the increased rent, but at all the other expenses we should certainly be led into. I countered all her fears by pretending I had a horror of anything temporary; I forced myself to believe in this feeling and deliberately exaggerated it. Certainly, the cost of furnishing and arranging the apartment would exceed our income for the present year, but our fortune, which was already large, was sure to increase still farther; I counted on my lectures for this, on the publication of my book and, such was my folly, on the profits from my new farms. In consequence, I stopped short at no expense, telling myself at each new one that here was another tie and thinking also that by these means I should suppress every vagabond inclination I felt – or feared I might feel – within me.

For the first few days, our time was taken up from morning to night by shopping and other business of the sort; and though eventually Marceline's brother very obligingly offered to do as much as he could for us, it was not long before Marceline felt thoroughly tired out. Then, as soon as we were settled in, instead of resting as she should have done, she felt obliged to receive visitors; they flocked to see us now because we had been absent from Paris during the first days of our marriage, and Marceline, who had become unused to society, was incapable of getting rid of them quickly or of shutting her doors altogether. When I came home in the evening, I found her exhausted, and, though her fatigue, which seemed only natural, caused me no anxiety, I did my best to lessen it; often receiving visits in her stead, which was very little to my taste, and sometimes paying them – which was still less so.

I have never been a brilliant talker; the frivolity, the wit, the spirit of fashionable drawing-rooms, were things in which I could take no pleasure; yet in old days I had frequented some of these salons – but how long ago that seemed! What had happened since then? In other people's company, I felt I was dull, gloomy, unwelcome, at once bored and boring . . . By a singular piece of ill-luck, you, whom I considered my only real friends, were absent from Paris and not expected back for long. Should I have been able to speak to you more openly? Would you have perhaps understood me better than I did myself? But what did I know at that time of all that was growing up within me, of all I am now telling you? The future seemed to be absolutely assured and I had never thought myself more master of it.

And even if I had been more perspicacious, what help against myself should I have found in Hubert, Didier, or Maurice, or in all the others whom you know and judge as I do? I very soon discovered, alas, the impossibility of their understanding me. In our very first conversations, I found myself forced to impersonate a false character, to resemble the man they imagined I still was; and for convenience sake, I pretended to have the thoughts and tastes with which they credited me. One cannot both be sincere and seem so.

I was rather more willing to renew my acquaintance with the people of my own profession – archaeologists and philologists – but I found very little more pleasure and no more emotion in talking to them than in consulting a good dictionary. I hoped at first to find a rather more direct comprehension of life in one or two novelists and poets; but if they really had such a comprehension, it must be confessed they did not show it; most of them, I thought, did not really live – contented themselves with appearing to live, and were on the verge of considering life merely as a vexatious hindrance to writing. I could not blame them for it; and I do not affirm that the mistake was not mine ... As to that, what did I mean by 'living'? That is exactly what I wanted to find out. One and another talked cleverly of the different events of life – never of what is at the back of them.

As for the few philosophers whose business it should have been to instruct me, I had long known what to expect of them; whether mathematicians or neo-Kantians, they kept as far away as possible from the disturbing reality and had no more concern for it than the algebraist has for the existence of the quantities he measures.

When I got back to Marceline, I did not conceal from her how tedious I found all these acquaintances.

'They are all alike,' I said to her. 'When I talk to one, I feel as if I were talking to the whole lot.'

'But, my dear,' said Marceline, 'you can't expect each of them to be different from all the others.'

'The greater their likeness to each other, the more unlike they are to me.'

And then I went on with a sigh, 'Not one of them has managed to be ill. They are alive – they seem to be alive, and yet not to know they are alive. For that matter, since I have been in their company, I have ceased to be alive myself. Today, amongst other days, what have I done? I had to leave you about nine o'clock. I had just a bare moment for a little reading before I went out; it was the only satisfactory moment of the day. Your brother was waiting for me at the solicitors, and after the solicitors, he insisted on sticking to me; I had to see the upholsterer with him; he was really a nuisance at the cabinet-makers and I only got rid of him at Gaston's; I had lunch in the neighbourhood with Philip and then I met Louis at a café and went with him to Theodore's absurd lecture, and paid him compliments when it was over; then, in order to get out of his invitation for Sunday, I had to go with him to Arthur's; then to a water-colour ex-hibition with Arthur; then left cards on Albertine and Julie ... I came in thoroughly exhausted and found you as tired as myself, after visits from Adeline, Marthe, Jeanne, and Sophie ... And now, in the even-ing, as I look back on my day, it seems to me so vain and so empty that I long to have it back and live it over again hour by hour – and the thought of it makes me inclined to weep.'

And yet I should not have been able to say what I meant by 'living', nor whether the very simple secret of my trouble was not that I had acquired a taste for a more spacious, breezier life, one that was less hemmed in, less regardful of others; the secret seemed to me much more mysterious than that; it was the secret, I thought, of one who had known death; for I moved a stranger among ordinary people, like a man who has risen from the grave, and at first I merely felt rather painfully out of my element; but soon I became aware of a very different feeling. I had known no pride, I repeat, when the publication of my Essay had brought me such praise. Was it pride now? Perhaps; but at any rate there was no trace of vanity mixed with it. It was rather, for the first time, the consciousness of my own worth. What separated me – distinguished me – from other people was crucial; what no one said, what no one could say but myself, *that* it was my task to say.

My lectures began soon after; the subject was congenial and I poured into the first of them all my newly born passion. Speaking of the later Latin civilization, I depicted artistic culture as welling up in a whole people, like a secretion, which is at first a sign of plethora, of a superabundance of health, but which afterwards stiffens, hardens, forbids the perfect contact of the mind with nature, hides under the persistent appearance of life a diminution of life, turns into an outside sheath, in which the cramped mind languishes and pines, in which at last it dies. Finally, pushing my thought to its logical conclusion, I showed Culture, born of life, as the destroyer of life.

The historians criticized a tendency, as they phrased it, to too rapid generalization. Other people blamed my method; and those who complimented me were those who understood me least.

*

It was at the end of my lecture that I came across Ménalque again for the first time. I had never seen much of him, and shortly before my marriage, he had started on one of those distant voyages of discovery which sometimes kept him from us for over a year. In the old days, I had never much liked him; he seemed proud and he took no interest in my existence. I was therefore astonished to see him at my first lecture. His very insolence, which had at first held me aloof from him, pleased me, and I thought the smile he gave me all the more charming because I knew he smiled rarely. Recently, an absurd – a shameful – lawsuit had caused a scandal and given the newspapers a convenient occasion to drag him through the mud; those whom he had offended by his disdain and superiority seized this pretext to revenge themselves; and what irritated them most was that he appeared not to care.

'One must allow other people to be right,' he used to say when he was insulted, 'it consoles them for not being anything else.'

But 'good society' was indignant and people who, as they say, 'respect themselves', thought it their duty to turn their backs on him, and so pay him back his contempt. This was an extra encouragement to me; feeling myself attracted by a secret influence, I went up to him and embraced him before everyone.

When they saw to whom I was talking the last intruders withdrew; I was left alone with Ménalque.

After the irritating criticisms and inept compliments I had been listening to, his few words on the subject of my lecture were very soothing.

'You are burning what you used to adore,' said he. 'Very good. It is a little late in the day, but never mind,

the fire is all the fiercer. I am not sure whether I altogether understand you. You make me curious. I don't
much care about talking, but I should like to talk to
you. Come and dine with me tonight.'

'Dear Ménalque,' I answered, 'you seem to forget
that I am married.'

'Yes,' he answered, 'quite true. The frank cordiality
with which you were not afraid to greet me made me
think you might be free.'

I was afraid I might have wounded him; still more so
of seeming weak, and I told him I would join him after
dinner.

*

Ménalque never did more than pass through Paris on
his way to somewhere else; he always stayed in a hotel.
On this occasion he had had several rooms fitted up for
him as a private apartment; he had his own servants,
took his meals apart, lived apart, stuffs and hangings of
great value which he had brought back from Nepal
had been hung on the walls and thrown over the furniture, whose commonplace ugliness was an offence
to him. He was dirtying them out, he said, before
presenting them to a museum. My haste to rejoin
him had been so great that I found him still at table
when I came in; as I excused myself for disturbing his
meal:

'But I have no intention of letting you disturb it,' he
said, 'and I expect you to let me finish it. If you had
come to dinner, I should have given you some Shiraz –
the wine that Hafiz celebrated – but it is too late now;
one must only drink if fasting; but you'll take some
liqueur, won't you?'

I accepted, thinking he would take some too, and

when only one glass was brought in, I expressed astonishment.

'Forgive me,' he said, 'but I hardly ever drink such things.'

'Are you afraid of getting drunk?'

'Oh!' replied he, 'on the contrary! But I consider sobriety a more powerful intoxication – in which I keep my lucidity.'

'And you pour the drink out for others?'

He smiled.

'I cannot,' said he, 'expect everyone to have my virtues. It's good enough to meet with my vices . . .'

'You smoke, at any rate?'

'No, not even that. Smoking is an impersonal, negative, too easily achieved kind of drunkenness; what I want from drunkenness is an enhancement, not a diminution of life. But that's enough. Do you know where I have just come from? Biskra. I heard you had been staying there, and I thought I would like to follow up your tracks. What could the blindfolded scholar, the learned bookworm have come to do at Biskra? It's my habit to be discreet only about things that are confided to me; for things that I find out myself, I'll admit that I have an unbounded curiosity. So I searched, poked about, questioned wherever I could. My indiscretion was rewarded, since it has made me wish to meet you again; since instead of the learned man of habit you seemed to be in the old days, I know now that you are . . . it's for you to tell me what.'

I felt myself blushing.

'What did you find out about me, Ménalque?'

'Do you want to know? But there's no need to be alarmed! You know your friends and mine well enough to be sure there is no one I can talk to about you. You saw how well your lecture was understood?'

'But,' said I, a little impatiently, 'there's nothing yet to prove that I can talk to you better than to them. Come on then! What is it you found out about me?'

'First of all, that you had been ill.'

'But there's nothing in that to ...'

'Oh, yes! That in itself is very important. Then I was told you liked going out alone, without a book (that's what started me wondering), or, when you were not alone, you preferred the company of children to that of your wife ... Don't blush like that, or I shan't go on.'

'Go on without looking at me.'

'One of the children – his name was Moktir, if I remember right – (I have scarcely ever seen a handsomer boy, and never a greater little swindler) seemed to have a good deal to say about you. I enticed him – I bribed him to confide in me ... not an easy thing to do, as you know, for I think it was only another lie, when he said he was not lying that time ... Tell me whether what he told me about you is true.'

In the meantime, Ménalque had got up and taken a little box out of a drawer.

'Are these scissors yours?' he said, opening the box and taking out a shapeless, twisted, rusty object, which, however, I had little difficulty in recognizing as the pair of scissors Moktir had purloined.

'Yes, they are; they were my wife's scissors.'

'He pretends he took them when your head was turned away one day he was alone in the room with you; but that's not the point; he pretends that at the moment he was hiding them in his burnous, he saw you

94

were watching him in the glass and caught the reflection of your eyes looking at him. You saw the theft and said nothing! Moktir was very much astonished at this silence – and so was I.'

'And I am too at what you have just said. What! Do you mean to say he knew I had caught him at it?'

'It isn't that that matters; you were trying to be more cunning than he; it's a game at which children like that will always get the better of us. You thought you had him, and in reality, it was he who had you . . . But that's not what matters. I should like an explanation of your silence.'

'I should like one myself.'

Some time passed without a word from either of us. Ménalque, who was pacing up and down the room, lighted a cigarette absent-mindedly and then immediately threw it away.

'The fact is,' said he, 'there's a "sense", as people say, a "sense" which seems to be lacking in you, my dear Michel.'

'The "moral sense",' said I, forcing myself to smile.

'Oh, no! simply the sense of property.'

'You don't seem to have much of it yourself.'

'I have so little of it that, as you see, nothing in this place is mine; not even – or rather, especially not, the bed I sleep on. I have a horror of rest; possessions encourage one to indulge in it, and there's nothing like security for making one fall asleep; I like life well enough to want to live it awake, and so, in the very midst of my riches, I maintain the sensation of a state of precariousness, by which means I aggravate, or at any rate intensify, my life. I will not say I like danger, but I like life to be hazardous, and I want it to demand at every moment the whole of my courage, my happiness, my health ...'

'Then what do you blame me for?' I interrupted.

'Oh, how little you understand me, my dear Michel; for once that I am foolish enough to try and make a profession of faith! ... If I care little for the approbation or disapprobation of men, Michel, it is not in order to approve or disapprove in my turn; those words have very little sense for me. I spoke of myself too much just now ... I was carried away by thinking you understood me ... I simply meant to say that, for a person who has not got the sense of property, you seem to possess a great deal. Isn't that rather serious?'

'And what is this great deal I possess?'

'Nothing, if you take it in that way ... But are you not beginning a course of lectures? Have you not an estate in Normandy? Have you not just settled yourself – and luxuriously too – in an apartment at Passy? You are married? Are you not expecting a child?'

'Well!' said I, impatiently, 'it merely proves that I have succeeded in making my life more dangerous than yours.'

'Yes, merely,' repeated Ménalque ironically; then, turning abruptly, he put out his hand:

'Well, good-bye now; I don't think any more talk tonight would be of much use. But I shall see you again soon.'

Some time went by before I saw him again.

*

Fresh work, fresh preoccupations took up my time; an Italian scholar brought to my notice some new documents he had discovered which were important for my lectures and which I had to study at some length. The feeling that my first lesson had been misunderstood stimulated me to shed a different and more powerful light on the succeeding ones; I was thus led to enunciate as a doctrine what I had at first only tentatively suggested as an ingenious hypothesis. How many assertions owe their strength to the lucky circumstance that as suggestions they were not understood? In my own case, I admit I cannot distinguish what proportion of obstinacy may have mingled with my natural propensity for asserting my opinions. The new things I had to say seemed to me especially urgent because of the difficulty of saying them, and above all of getting them understood.

But, alas, how pale words become, when compared with deeds! Was not Ménalque's life, Ménalque's slightest action a thousand times more eloquent than my lectures? How well I understood now that the great philosophers of antiquity, whose teaching was almost wholly moral, worked by example as much – even more than by precept!

*

The next time I saw Ménalque was in my own house, nearly three weeks after our first meeting. We had been giving a crowded evening party, and he came in almost at the end of it. In order to avoid being continually disturbed, Marceline and I had settled to be at home on Thursday's; in this way it was easier to keep our doors shut for the rest of the week. Every Thursday evening then, those people who called themselves our friends used to come and see us; our rooms were large enough to hold a good many guests and they used to stay late. I think that what attracted them most was Marceline's exquisite charm and the pleasure of talking to each other, for as to myself, from the very beginning of these parties, there was nothing I could find either to say or to listen to, and it was with difficulty I concealed my boredom.

That evening, I was wandering aimlessly from the drawing-room to the smoking-room, from the ante-chamber to the library, caught by a sentence here and there, observing very little but looking about me more or less vaguely.

Antoine, Étienne, and Godefroi were discussing the last vote in the Chamber, as they lolled on my wife's elegant armchairs. Hubert and Louis were carelessly looking through some fine etchings from my father's collection, entirely regardless of how they were creasing them. In the smoking-room, Mathias, the better to listen to Leonard, had put his red-hot cigar down on a rosewood table. A glass of curaçoa had been spilt on the carpet. Albert was sprawling impudently on a sofa, with his muddy boots dirtying the cover. And the very dust of the air one breathed came from the horrible wear and tear of material objects ... A frantic desire seized me to send all my guests packing. Furniture, stuffs, prints, lost all their value for me at the first stain; things stained were things touched by disease, with the mark of death on them. I wanted to save them, to lock them up in a cupboard for my own use alone. How lucky Ménalque is, thought I, to have no possessions! The reason I suffer is that I want to preserve things. But after all, what does it really matter to me? ...

There was a small, less brilliantly lighted drawing-room, partitioned off by a transparent glass door, and there Marceline was receiving some of her more

intimate friends; she was half reclining on a pile of cush-
ions and looked so fearfully pale and tired that I
suddenly took fright and vowed that this reception
should be the last. It was already late. I was beginning
to take out my watch, when I suddenly felt Moktir's
little scissors in my pocket.

'Why did the little wretch steal them,' thought I, 'if
it was only to spoil and destroy them at once?'

At that moment someone touched me on the shoulder; I turned quickly; it was Ménalque.

He was almost the only person in evening dress. He
had just arrived. He asked me to present him to my
wife; I should certainly not have done so of my own
accord. Ménalque was distinguished looking – almost
handsome; his face was like a pirate's, barred by an
enormous drooping moustache, already quite grey;
his eyes shone with a cold flame that denoted courage
and decision rather than kindness. He was no sooner
standing before Marceline than I knew she had taken a
dislike to him. After he had exchanged a few banal
words of courtesy with her, I carried him off to the
smoking-room.

I had heard that very morning of the new mission on
which the Colonial Office was sending him; the newspapers, as they recalled his adventurous career, seemed
to have forgotten their recent base insults and now
could find no words fine enough to praise him with.
Each was more eager than the other to extol and exaggerate his services to his country, to the whole of
humanity, as if he never undertook anything but with a
humanitarian purpose; and they quoted examples of
his abnegation, his devotion, his courage, as if such
encomiums might be considered a reward.

I began to congratulate him, but he interrupted me at the first words.

'What! You too, my dear Michel! But *you* didn't begin by insulting me,' said he. 'Leave all that nonsense to the papers. They seem to be surprised that a man with a certain reputation can still have any virtues at all. They establish distinctions and reserves which I cannot apply to myself, for I exist only as a whole; my only claim is to be natural, and the pleasure I feel in an action, I take as a sign that I ought to do it.'

'That may lead far,' I said.

'Indeed I hope so,' answered Ménalque. 'If only the people we know could persuade themselves of the truth of this! But most of them believe that it is only by constraint they can get any good out of themselves, and so they live in a state of psychological distortion. It is his own self that each of them is most afraid of resembling. Each of them sets up a pattern and imitates it; he doesn't even choose the pattern he imitates: he accepts a pattern that has been chosen for him. And yet I verily believe there are other things to be read in man. But people don't dare to – they don't dare to turn the page. Laws of imitation! Laws of fear, I call them. The fear of finding oneself alone – that is what they suffer from – and so they don't find themselves at all. I detest such moral agoraphobia – the most odious cowardice I call it. Why, one always has to be alone to invent anything – but they don't want to invent anything. The part in each of us that we feel is different from other people is just the part that is rare, the part that makes our special value – and that is the very thing people try to suppress. They go on imitating. And yet they think they love life.'

I let Ménalque speak on; he was saying exactly what I myself had said the month before to Marceline; I ought to have approved him. For what reason, through what moral cowardice did I interrupt him and say, in imitation of Marceline, the very sentence word for word with which she had interrupted me then?

'But, my dear Ménalque, you can't expect each one of them to be different from all the others.' ...

Ménalque stopped speaking abruptly, looked at me oddly, and then, as at that very moment Eusèbe came up to take leave, he unceremoniously turned his back on me and went off to talk about some trifle or other to Hector.

The words were no sooner out of my mouth than I realized not only that they were stupid, but worse still, that they might have given Ménalque the impression that I thought his remarks had been pointed at me. It was late; my guests were leaving. When the drawing-room was nearly empty, Ménalque came back to me.

'I can't leave you like this,' he said. 'No doubt, I misunderstood what you said. Let me at least hope so.'

'No,' I answered, 'you did not misunderstand it ... but it was senseless, and I had no sooner said it than I knew it was foolish. I was sorry, and especially sorry to think it would make you place me among the very people you were attacking and who, I assure you, are as odious to me as to you. I hate people of principle.'

'Yes,' answered Ménalque, laughing, 'there is nothing more detestable in the world. It is impossible to expect any sort of sincerity from them; for they never do anything but what their principles have decreed they should do; or if they do, they think they have done wrong. At the mere suspicion you might be one of them, the words froze on my lips. I felt by my distress what a great affection I have for you; I hoped I was mistaken – not in my affection, but in the conclusion I had drawn.'

'Yes, really; your conclusion was wrong.'

'Oh! it was, I am sure,' said he, suddenly taking my hand. 'Listen a moment; I shall soon be going away, but I should like to see you again. My expedition this time will be a longer one and more risky than any of the others; I don't know when I shall come back. I must start in a fortnight's time; no one knows I am leaving so soon; I tell you so in confidence. I start at day-break. The night before leaving is always a night of terrible heartache for me. Give me a proof that you are not a man of principle; may I count on it that you will spend that last night with me?'

'But we shall see each other again before then,' I said, a little astonished.

'No; during the next fortnight I shall be at home to no one. I shall not even be in Paris. Tomorrow I leave for Budapest; in six days' time I must be in Rome. I have friends dotted here and there to whom I must say good-bye before leaving. There is one expecting me in Madrid.'

'Very well then, I will pass your night of vigil with you.'

'And we will have some Shiraz to drink,' said Ménalque.

A few days after this party, Marceline began to feel less well. I have already said she was easily tired; but she did not complain, and as I attributed her fatigue to her condition, I thought it natural and felt no particular anxiety. A rather foolish – or rather ignorant – old doctor had at first been over-reassuring. Some fresh symptoms, however, accompanied by fever, decided me to send for Dr Tr—, who was considered at that time the cleverest specialist in Paris for such cases. He expressed astonishment that I had not called him in sooner and prescribed a strict régime which she ought to have begun to follow some time ago. Marceline had been very courageous, but not very prudent, and had overtired herself. She was told she must now lie up till the date of her confinement, which was expected about the end of January. Feeling no doubt a little anxious and more unwell than she would admit, Marceline consented very meekly to the most tiresome orders. She had a moment's rebellion, however, when Tr— prescribed quinine in such heavy doses that she knew it might endanger the child. For three days she obstinately refused to take it; then as her fever increased she was obliged to submit to that too; but this time it was with deep sadness and as if she were mournfully giving up all hope of the future; the resolution which had hitherto sustained her seemed broken down by a kind of religious resignation, and her condition grew suddenly worse in the days that followed.

I tended her with greater care than ever, did my best to reassure her and repeated the very words Dr Tr— had used, that he could see nothing very serious in her case; but her extreme anxiety ended by alarming me too. Alas! our happiness was already resting on the dangerous foundations of hope – and hope of what an uncertain future! I, who at first had taken pleasure only in the past, may have one day felt, thought I, the sudden and intoxicating sweetness of a fugitive moment, but the future disenchants the present even more than the present then disenchanted the past; and since our night at Sorrento my whole love, my whole life have been projected into the future.

*

In the meantime the evening I had promised Ménalque came round; and notwithstanding the reluctance I felt at abandoning Marceline for a whole winter's night, I got her, as best I could, to acknowledge the solemnity of the occasion and the gravity of my promise. Marceline was a little better that evening and yet I was anxious; a nurse took my place beside her. But as soon as I was in the street, my anxiety gained ground; I shook it off, struggled against it, was angry with myself for not being better able to get rid of it; thus I gradually reached a state of excessive tension, of singular excitement, both very unlike and very like the painful uneasiness from which it sprang, but liker still to happiness. It was late and I strode along rapidly; the snow began to fall in thick flakes; I was glad to be breathing a keener air, to be struggling with the cold; I was happy with the wind, the night, the snow against me; I rejoiced in my strength.

Ménalque had heard me coming and came out on to the landing to welcome me. He was waiting for me not without impatience. His face was pale and he looked overwrought. He helped me off with my overcoat and forced me to change my wet boots for some soft Persian slippers. Sweets and cakes were standing on a small table by the fire. There were two lamps, but the light in the room came chiefly from the fire on the hearth. Ménalque immediately inquired after Marceline; for the sake of simplicity I answered that she was very well.

'Are you expecting your child soon?' he went on.

'In a month.'

Ménalque bent down towards the fire as if he wished to hide his face. He remained silent. He remained silent so long that at last I felt embarrassed, and as I myself could think of nothing to say either, I got up, took a few steps, and then went up to him and put my hand on his shoulder. Presently, as though he were pursuing his thoughts aloud:

'One must choose,' he murmured. 'The chief thing is to know what one wants . . .'

'Don't you want to go?' I asked, in some uncertainty as to what he meant.

'It looks like it.'

'Are you hesitating then?'

'What is the use? You have a wife and child, so stay at home . . . Of the thousand forms of life, each of us can know but one. It is madness to envy other people's happiness; one would not know what to do with it. Happiness won't come to one ready-made; it has to be made to measure. I am going away tomorrow; yes, I know; I have tried to cut out my happiness to fit me . . . keep your calm happiness of hearth and home . . .'

'*I* cut out my happiness to fit me too,' I said, 'but I have grown; I am not at ease in my happiness now; sometimes I think it is strangling me . . .'

'Pooh! you'll get accustomed to it!' said Ménalque. Then he planted himself in front of me and looked deep into my eyes; as I found nothing to say, he smiled rather sadly.

'One imagines one possesses and in reality one is possessed,' he went on. 'Pour yourself out a glass of Shiraz, dear Michel; you won't often taste it; and eat some of those rose-coloured sweets which the Persians take with it. I shall drink with you this evening, forget that I am leaving tomorrow, and talk as if the night were long . . . Do you know the reason why poetry and philosophy are nothing but dead-letter nowadays? It is because they have severed themselves from life. In Greece, ideas went hand in hand with life; so that the artist's life itself was already a poetic realization, the philosopher's life a putting into action of his philosophy; in this way, as both philosophy and poetry took part in life, instead of remaining unacquainted with each other, philosophy provided food for poetry, and poetry gave expression to philosophy – and the result was admirably persuasive. Nowadays beauty no longer acts; action no longer desires to be beautiful; and wisdom works in a sphere apart.'

'But *you* live your wisdom,' said I; 'why do you not write your memoirs? Or simply,' I added, seeing him smile, 'recollections of your travels?'

'Because I do not want to recollect,' he replied. 'I should be afraid of preventing the future and of allowing the past to encroach on me. It is out of the utter forgetfulness of yesterday that I create every new hour's freshness. It is never enough for me to have been happy. I do not believe in dead things and cannot distinguish between being no more and never having been.'

These words were too far in advance of my thoughts not to end by irritating me; I should have liked to hang back, to stop him; but I tried in vain to contradict, and besides I was more irritated with myself than with Ménalque. I remained silent therefore, while he, sometimes pacing up and down like a wild beast in a cage, sometimes stooping over the fire, kept up a long and moody silence, or again broke abruptly into words:

'If only our paltry minds,' he said, 'were able to embalm our memories! But memories keep badly. The most delicate fade and shrivel; the most voluptuous decay; the most delicious are the most dangerous in the end. The things one repents of were at first delicious.'

Again a long silence; and then he went on:

'Regrets, remorse, repentance, are past joys seen from behind. I don't like looking backwards and I leave my past behind me as the bird leaves his shade to fly away. Oh, Michel! every joy is always awaiting us, but it must always be the only one; it insists on finding the bed empty and demands from us a widower's welcome. Oh, Michel! every joy is like the manna of the desert which corrupts from one day to the next; it is like the fountain of Ameles, whose waters, says Plato, could never be kept in any vase ... Let every moment carry away with it all that it brought.'

Ménalque went on speaking for long; I cannot repeat all his words; but many of them were imprinted on my mind the more deeply, the more anxious I was to forget them; not that they taught me much that was new – but they suddenly laid bare my thoughts – thoughts I had shrouded in so many coverings that I had almost hoped to smother them.

And so the night of watching passed.

The next morning, after I had seen Ménalque into the train that carried him away, as I was walking home on my way back to Marceline, I felt horribly sad and full of hatred of his cynical joy; I wanted to believe it was a sham; I tried to deny it. I was angry with myself for not having found anything to say to him in reply; for having said words that might make him doubt my happiness, my love. And I clung to my doubtful happiness – my 'calm happiness', as Ménalque had called it; I could not, it was true, banish uneasiness from it, but I assured myself that uneasiness was the very food of love. I imagined the future and saw my child smiling at me; for his sake I would strengthen my character, I would build it up anew ... Yes, I walked with a confident step.

Alas! when I got in that morning, I was struck by a sight of unaccustomed disorder. The nurse met me and told me guardedly that my wife had been seized in the night with bad sickness and pains, though she did not think the term of her confinement was at hand; feeling very ill, she had sent for the doctor; he had arrived post-haste in the night and had not yet left the patient; then, seeing me change colour, I suppose, she tried to reassure me, said that things were going much better now, that ... I rushed to Marceline's room.

The room was darkened and at first I could make out nothing but the doctor, who signed to me to be quiet; then I saw a figure in the dark I did not know. Anxiously, noiselessly, I drew near the bed. Marceline's eyes were shut; she was so terribly pale that at first I thought she was dead; but she turned her head towards me, though without opening her eyes. The unknown figure was in a dark corner of the room, arranging, hiding, various objects; I saw shining instruments, cotton wool; I saw, I thought I saw a cloth stained with blood ... I felt I was tottering. I almost fell into the doctor's arms; he held me up. I understood; I was afraid of understanding ...

'The child?' I asked anxiously.

He shrugged his shoulders sadly. I lost all sense of what I was doing and flung myself sobbing against the bed. Oh! how suddenly the future had come upon me! The ground had given way abruptly beneath my feet; there was nothing there but an empty hole into which I stumbled headlong.

*

My recollections here are lost in dark confusion. Marceline, however, seemed at first to recover fairly quickly. The Christmas holidays allowed me a little respite and I was able to spend nearly the whole day with her. I read or wrote in her room, or read aloud to her quietly. I never went out without bringing her back flowers. I remembered the tenderness with which she had nursed me when I was ill, and surrounded her with so much love that sometimes she smiled as though it made her happy. Not a word was exchanged about the melancholy accident that had shattered our hopes . . .

Then phlebitis declared itself; and when that got better, a clot of blood suddenly set her hovering between life and death. It was night time; I remember leaning over her, feeling my heart stop and go on again with hers. How many nights I watched by her bedside, my eyes obstinately fixed on her, hoping by the strength of my love to instil some of my own life into hers. I no longer thought much about happiness; my single melancholy pleasure was sometimes seeing Marceline smile.

My lectures had begun again. How did I find strength to prepare them, to deliver them? . . . My memory of this time is blurred; I have forgotten how the weeks passed. And yet there was a little incident I must tell you about.

It was one morning, a little after the embolism; I was sitting with Marceline; she seemed a little better, but she was still ordered to keep absolutely motionless; she was not allowed to move even her arms. I bent over her to give her some drink and after she had drunk, and as I was still stooping over her, she begged me, in a voice made weaker still by her emotion, to open a little box, which she showed me by the direction of her glance; it was close by, on the table; I opened it and found it full of ribbons, bits of lace, little ornaments of no value ... I wondered what she wanted. I brought the box to her bedside and took out every object one by one. Was it this? That? ... No, not yet; and I felt her getting agitated.

'Oh, Marceline, is it this little rosary you want?'

She tried to smile.

'Are you afraid then that I shan't nurse you properly?'

'Oh, my dear,' she murmured. And I remembered our conversation at Biskra, and her timid reproaches when she heard me refuse what she called 'the help of God'.

I went on a little roughly: '*I* got well alone all right.'

'I prayed for you so much,' she answered.

She said the words tenderly, sadly. There was something anxious and imploring in her look ... I took the rosary and slipped it into her weak hand as it lay on the sheet beside her. A tearful, love-laden glance rewarded me – but I could not answer it; I waited another moment or two, feeling awkward and embarrassed;

finally, not knowing what to do, I said, 'Good-bye,' and left the room, with a feeling of hostility, and as though I had been turned out of it.

*

Meanwhile the horrible clot had brought on serious trouble; after her heart had escaped, it attacked her lungs, brought on congestion, impeded her breathing, made it short and laborious. I thought she would never get well. Disease had taken hold of Marceline, never again to leave her; it had marked her, stained her. Henceforth she was a thing that had been spoiled.

3

THE weather was now becoming warmer. As soon as
my lectures were over, I took Marceline to La Morinière, the doctor having told me that all immediate danger was past and that nothing would be more likely to
complete her cure than a change to purer air. I myself
was in great need of rest. The nights I had spent nurs-
ing her, almost entirely by myself, the prolonged
anxiety, and especially the kind of physical sympathy
which had made me at the time of her attack feel the
fearful throbbing of her heart in my own breast – all
this had exhausted me as much as if I myself had been ill.

I should have preferred to take Marceline to the
mountains, but she expressed the strongest desire to
return to Normandy, declared that no climate could be
better for her and reminded me that I must not neglect
the two farms of which I had rather rashly assumed the
charge. She insisted that as I had made myself responsible for them, it was my business to make them succeed. No sooner had we arrived therefore, than she
urged me to visit the estate immediately . . . I am not
sure that her friendly insistence did not go with a good
deal of abnegation; she was afraid, perhaps, that as she
still required assistance, I might think myself bound to
stay with her and not feel as free as I might wish to . . .
Marceline was better however; the colour had returned
to her cheeks, and nothing gave me greater comfort
than to feel her smile was less sad; I was able to leave
her without uneasiness.

I went then to the farms. The first hay was being

made. The scented air, heavy with pollen, at first went to my head like a strong drink. I felt that I had hardly breathed at all since last year, or breathed nothing but dust, so drowned was I in the honeyed sweetness of the atmosphere. The bank on which I seated myself in a kind of intoxication overlooked the house; I saw its blue roofs; I saw the still waters of the moat; all around were fields, some newly mown, others rich with grass; farther on, the curve of the brook; farther again, the woods where last autumn I had so often gone riding with Charles. A sound of singing, which I had been listening to for the last moment or two, drew near; it was the haymakers going home, with a fork or a rake on their shoulders. I recognized nearly all of them, and the unpleasant recollection came to me that I was not there as an enchanted traveller, but as their master. I went up to them, smiled, spoke to them, inquired after each of them in turn. Bocage that morning had already given me a report of the crops; he had indeed kept me regularly informed by letter of everything that went on in the farms. They were not doing so badly – much better than Bocage had led me to expect. But my arrival was being awaited in order to take some important decisions, and during the next few days I devoted myself to farm business to the best of my ability – not taking much pleasure in it, but hoping by this semblance of work to give some stability to my disintegrated life.

As soon as Marceline was well enough to receive visitors, a few friends came to stay with us. They were affectionate, quiet people, and Marceline liked their society, but it had the effect of making me leave the house with more pleasure than usual. I preferred the society of the farm hands; I felt that with them there was more to be learned – not that I questioned them – no; and I hardly know how to express the kind of rapture I felt when I was with them; I seemed to feel things with their senses rather than with my own – and while I knew what our friends were going to say before they opened their mouths, the mere sight of these poor fellows filled me with perpetual amazement.

If at first they appeared as condescending in their answers as I tried to avoid being in my questions, they soon became more tolerant of my presence. I came into closer contact with them. Not content with following them at their work, I wanted to see them at their play; their obtuse thoughts had little interest for me, but I shared their meals, listened to their jokes, fondly watched their pleasures. By a kind of sympathy similar to that which made my heart throb at the throbs of Marceline's, their alien sensations immediately awoke the echo of my own – no vague echo, but a sharp and precise one. I felt my own arms grow stiff with the mower's stiffness; I was weary with his weariness; the mouthful of cider he drank quenched my thirst; I felt it slip down his throat; one day, one of them, while sharpening his scythe, cut his thumb badly; his pain hurt me to the bone.

And it seemed to me that it was no longer with my sight alone that I became aware of the landscape, but that I *felt* it as well by some sense of touch, which my curious power of sympathy illimitably enlarged.

Bocage's presence was now a nuisance to me; when he came I had to play the master, which I had no longer the least inclination to do. I still gave orders – I had to – still superintended the labourers; but I no longer went on horseback, for fear of looking down on them from too great a height. But notwithstanding the precautions I took to accustom them to my presence and prevent them from feeling ill at ease in it, in theirs I was still filled as before with an evil curiosity. There was a mystery about the existence of each one of them. I always felt that a part of their lives was concealed. What did they do when I was not there? I refused to believe that they had not better ways of amusing themselves. And I credited each of them with a secret which I pertinaciously tried to discover. I went about prowling, following, spying. For preference I fastened on the rudest and roughest among them, as if I expected to find a guiding light shine from their darkness.

One in particular attracted me; he was fairly good-looking, tall, not in the least stupid, but wholly guided by instinct, never acting but on the spur of the moment, blown hither and thither by every passing impulse. He did not belong to the place, and had been taken on by some chance. An excellent worker for two days – and on the third dead drunk. One night I crept furtively down to the barn to see him; he lay sprawling in a heavy, drunken sleep. I stayed looking at him a long time ... One fine day, he went as he had come. How much I should have liked to know along what roads! ... I learned that same evening that Bocage had dismissed him.

I was furious with Bocage and sent for him.

'It seems you have dismissed Pierre,' I began. 'Will you kindly tell me why?'

He was a little taken aback by my anger, though I tried to moderate it.

'You didn't want to keep a dirty drunkard, did you,

Sir? A fellow who led all our best men into mischief!'

'It's my business to know the men I want to keep, not yours.'

'A regular waster! No one knew where he came from. It gave the place a bad name . . . If he had set fire to the barn one night, you mightn't have been so pleased, Sir.'

'That's my affair, I tell you. It's my farm, isn't it? I mean to manage it in my own way. In the future, be so good as to give me your reasons before dismissing people.'

Bocage, as I have told you, had known me since my childhood. However wounding my tone, he was too much attached to me to be much offended. He did not, in fact, take me sufficiently seriously. The Normandy peasant is too often disinclined to believe anything of which he cannot fathom the motive – that is to say, anything not prompted by interest. Bocage simply considered this quarrel as a piece of absurdity.

I did not want, however, to break off the conversation on a note of blame; feeling I had been too sharp with him, I cast about for something pleasant to add.

'Isn't your son Charles coming back soon?' I ended by asking after a moment's silence.

'I thought you had quite forgotten him, Sir; you seemed to trouble your head about him so little,' said Bocage, still rather hurt.

'Forget him, Bocage! How could I, after all we did together last year? I'm counting on him in fact to help me with the farms . . .'

'You're very good, Sir. Charles is coming home in a week's time.'

'Well, I'm glad to hear it, Bocage,' and I dismissed him.

Bocage was not far wrong; I had not of course forgotten Charles, but I now cared very little about him. How can I explain that after such vehement camaraderie, my feeling for him now should be so flat and spiritless? The fact is my occupations and tastes were no longer the same as last year. My two farms, I must admit, did not interest me so much as the people employed on them; and if I wanted to foregather with them, Charles would be very much in the way. He was far too reasonable and too respectable. So notwithstanding the vivid and delightful memories I kept of him, I looked forward with some apprehension to his return.

He returned – and how right Ménalque was to repudiate all memories! There entered the room in Charles's place an absurd individual with a bowler hat. Heavens! how changed he was! Embarrassed and constrained though I felt, I tried not to respond too frigidly to the joy he showed at seeing me again; but even his joy was disagreeable to me; it was awkward, and I thought insincere. I received him in the drawing-room, and as it was late and dark, I could hardly distinguish his face; but when the lamp was brought in, I saw with disgust he had let his whiskers grow.

The conversation that evening was more or less dreary; then, as I knew he would be continually at the farms, I avoided going down to them for almost a week, and fell back on my studies and the society of my guests. And as soon as I began to go out again, I was absorbed by a totally new occupation.

Wood-cutters had invaded the woods. Every year a

part of the timber on the estate was sold; the woods were marked off into twelve equal lots which were cut in rotation and every year furnished, besides a few fully grown trees, a certain amount of twelve-year-old copse wood for faggots.

This work was done in the winter, and the wood-cutters were obliged by contract to have the ground cleared before spring. But old Heurtevent, the timber-merchant who directed operations, was so slack that sometimes spring came upon the copses while the wood was still lying on the ground; fresh, delicate shoots could then be seen forcing their way upwards through the dead branches, and when at last the wood-cutters cleared the ground, it was not without destroying many of the young saplings.

That year old Heurtevent's remissness was even greater than we had looked for. In the absence of any other bidder, I had been obliged to let him have the copse wood exceedingly cheap; so that being assured in any case of a handsome profit, he took very little pains to dispose of the timber which had cost him so little. And from week to week he put off the work with various excuses – a lack of labourers, or bad weather, or a sick horse, or an urgent call for work elsewhere, and so on – with the result that as late as the middle of summer, none of it had been removed.

The year before, this would have irritated me to the highest degree; this year it left me fairly calm; I saw well enough the damage Heurtevent was causing me; but the devastated woods were beautiful; it gave me pleasure to wander in them, tracking and watching the game, startling the snakes, and sometimes sitting by the hour on one of the fallen trunks which still seemed to continue living, with green shoots springing from its wounds.

Then suddenly, about the middle of the last fortnight in August, Heurtevent made up his mind to send his men. Six of them came with orders to finish the work in ten days. The part of the woods that had been cut was that bordering on La Valterie; it was arranged that the wood-cutters should have their food brought them from the farm, in order to expedite the work. The labourer chosen for this task was a curious young rascal called Bute; he had just come back from a term of military service which had utterly demoralized him; but physically, he was in admirable condition; he was one of the farm hands I most enjoyed talking to. By this arrangement I was able to see him without going down to the farm. For it was just at that time that I began going out again. For a few days I hardly left the woods except for my meals at La Morinière, and I was very often late for them. I pretended I had to superintend the work, though in reality I only went to see the workers.

Sometimes two of Heurtevent's sons joined the batch of six men; one was about twenty, the other about fifteen years old, long-limbed, wiry, hard-featured young fellows. They had a foreign look about them, and I learned later that their mother was actually a Spanish woman. I was astonished at first that she should have travelled to such distant parts, but Heurtevent had been a rolling stone in his youth and had, it appears, married her in Spain. For this reason he was rather looked askance at in the neighbourhood. The first time I saw the younger of the sons was, I remember, on a rainy day; he was alone, sitting on a very high cart, on the top of a great pile of faggots. He was lolling back among the branches, and singing, or rather shouting, a kind of extraordinary song, which was like nothing I had ever heard in our parts. The cart-horses knew the road and followed it without any guidance from him. I cannot tell you the effect this song had on me; for I had never heard its like except in Africa ... The boy looked excited – drunk; when I passed, he did not even glance at me. The next day, I learned he was a son of Heurtevent's. It was in order to see him, or rather in the hopes of seeing him, that I spent so much time in the copse. The men by now had very nearly finished clearing it. The young Heurtevents came only three times. They seemed proud and I could not get a word out of them.

Bute, on the other hand, liked talking; I soon managed to make him understand that there was nothing it was not safe to say to me. Upon this he let himself go and soon stripped the countryside of every rag of respectability. I lapped up his mysterious secrets with avidity. They surpassed my expectation and yet at the same time failed to satisfy me. Was this what was really grumbling below the surface of appearances or was it merely another kind of hypocrisy? No matter! I questioned Bute as I had questioned the uncouth chronicles of the Goths. Fumes of the abyss rose darkly from his stories and as I breathed them uneasily and fearfully, my head began to turn. He told me to begin with that Heurtevent had relations with his daughter. I was afraid if I showed the slightest disapprobation I should put an end to his confidences; curiosity spurred me on.

'And the mother? Doesn't she object?'

'The mother! She has been dead full twelve years … He used to beat her.'

'How many are there in the family?'

'Five children. You've seen the eldest son and the youngest. There's another of sixteen who's delicate and wants to turn priest. And then the eldest daughter has already had two children by the father.'

And little by little I learned a good deal more, so that do what I would, my imagination began to circle round the lurid attractions of Heurtevent's house like a blow-fly round a putrid piece of meat. One night the eldest son had tried to rape a young servant girl, and as she struggled, the father had intervened to help his son and had held her with his huge hands, while the second son went piously on with his prayers on the floor above, and the youngest looked on at the drama as an amused spectator. As far as the rape is concerned, I imagine it was not very difficult, for Bute went on to say that not long after, the servant girl, having acquired a taste for this sort of thing, had tried to seduce the young priest.

'And hasn't she succeeded?' I asked.

'He hasn't given in so far, but he's a bit wobbly,' answered Bute.

'Didn't you say there was another daughter?'

'Yes; she picks up as many fellows as she can lay hold of. And all for nothing too. When she's set on it, she wouldn't mind paying herself. But you mustn't carry on at her father's. He would give you what for. He says you can do as you like in your own house, but don't let other people come nosing round! Pierre, the farm hand you sent away, got a nasty knock on the head one night, though he held his tongue

121

about it. Since then, she has her chaps in the home woods.'

'Have you had a go yourself?' I asked with an encouraging look.

He dropped his eyes for form's sake and said, chuckling:

'Every now and then.' Then, raising his eyes quickly, 'So has old Bocage's boy,' he added.

'What boy is that?'

'Alcide, the one who sleeps at the farm. Surely you know him, Sir?'

I was simply astounded to hear Bocage had another son.

'It is true,' went on Bute, 'that last year he was still at his uncle's. But it's very odd you've never met him in the woods, Sir; he poaches in them nearly every night.'

Bute said these last words in a lower voice. He looked at me and I saw it was essential to smile. Then Bute seemed satisfied and went on:

'Good Lord, Sir, of course you know your woods are poached. They're so big it doesn't do much harm to anyone.'

I looked so far from being displeased that Bute was emboldened to go on, and I think now he was glad to do Bocage an ill turn. He pointed out one or two hollows in the ground in which Alcide had set his snares, and then showed me a place in the hedge where I should be almost certain of catching him. It was a boundary hedge and ran along the top of a bank; there was a narrow opening in it through which Alcide was in the habit of coming about six o'clock in the evening. At this place Bute and I amused ourselves by stretching a copper wire which we very neatly concealed. Then, having made me swear not to give him away, Bute departed.

For three evenings I waited in vain. I began to think Bute had played me a trick ... At last on the fourth evening, I heard a light step approaching. My heart began to beat and I had a sudden revelation of the horrible allurement of the poacher's life ... The snare was so well set that Alcide walked straight into it. I saw him suddenly fall flat, with his ankle caught in the wire. He tried to save himself, fell down again, and began struggling like a trapped rabbit. But I had hold of him in an instant. He was a wicked looking youngster, with green eyes, tow-coloured hair and a ferrety expression. He started kicking; then, as I held him so tight that he was unable to move, he tried to bite; and when that failed, he spat out the most extraordinary volley of abuse I have ever heard. In the end I could resist no longer and burst out laughing. At this, he stopped abruptly, looked at me, and went on in a lower tone:

'You brute, you! You've hurt me something horrible.'

'Show me where.'

He slipped his stocking down over his boot and showed me his ankle, where a slight pink mark was just visible.

'It's nothing at all.'

He smiled a little; then, 'I shall tell Father,' he said in a cunning voice, 'that it's *you* who set snares.'

'Why, good Heavens, it's one of your own!'

'Sure enough, you never set that one.'

'Why do you say that?'

'You would never know how to set them as well as that. Just show me how you did it.'

'Give me a lesson . . .'

That evening I came in very late for dinner; no one knew where I was and Marceline had been anxious. But I did not tell her I had set six snares and so far from scolding Alcide had given him ten sous.

The next evening when I went with him to visit the snares, much to my entertainment I found two rabbits caught in them. Of course I let him take them. The shooting season had not yet begun. I wondered what became of the game, as it was impossible to dispose of it openly without the risk of getting into trouble. Alcide refused to tell me. Finally, I learned, through Bute again, that Heurtevent was the receiver and his youngest son the go-between between Alcide and him. Was this going to give me an opportunity of a deeper insight into the secrets of that mysterious, unapproachable family? With what passionate eagerness I set about poaching!

I met Alcide every evening; we caught great numbers of rabbits and once even a young roe-deer which still showed some faint signs of life; I cannot recall without horror the delight Alcide took in killing it. We put the deer in a place of safety from which young Heurtevent could take it away at night.

From that moment I no longer cared for going out in the day, when there was so little to attract me in the emptied woods. I even tried to work – melancholy, purposeless work, for I had resigned my temporary lectureship – thankless, dreary work, from which I would be suddenly distracted by the slightest song, the slightest sound coming from the country outside; in every passing cry I heard an invitation. How often I have leapt from my reading and run to the window to see – nothing pass by! How often I have hurried out of doors ... The only attention I found possible was that of my five senses.

But when night fell – and it was the season now when night falls early – that was our hour. I had never before guessed its beauty; and I stole out of doors as a thief steals in. I had trained my eyes to be like a night-bird's. I wondered to see the grass taller and more easily stirred, the trees denser. The dark gave every-thing fresh dimensions, made the ground look distant, lent every surface the quality of depth. The smoothest path looked dangerous. Everywhere one felt the awakening of creatures that lead a life of darkness.

'Where does your father think you are now?'

'In the stables looking after the cattle.'

Alcide slept there, I knew, close to the pigeons and the hens; as he was locked in at night, he used to creep out by a hole in the roof. There still hung about his clothes a steamy odour of fowls.

Then, as soon as the game had been collected, he would disappear abruptly into the dark, as if down a trap-door – without a sign of farewell, without a word of tomorrow's rendezvous. I knew that before return-ing to the farm, where the dogs recognized him and kept silent, he used to meet the Heurtevent boy and deliver his goods. But where? Try as I might, I was never able to find out; threats, bribes, cunning – all failed; the Heurtevents remained inaccessible. I cannot say where my folly showed more triumphantly. Was it in this pursuit of a trivial mystery, which constantly eluded me – or had I even invented the mystery by the mere force of my curiosity? But what did Alcide do when he left me? Did he really sleep at the farm? Or did he simply make the farmer think so? My compromising myself was utterly useless; I merely succeeded in lessening his respect without increasing his confidence – and it both infuriated and distressed me.

After he had disappeared, I suddenly felt myself horribly alone; I went back across the fields, through the dew-drenched grass, my head reeling with darkness, with lawlessness, with anarchy; dripping, muddy, covered with leaves. In the distance there shone from the sleeping house, guiding me like a peaceful beacon, the lamp I had left alight in my study, where Marceline thought I was working, or the lamp of Marceline's own bedroom. I had persuaded her that I should not have been able to sleep without first going out in this way. It was true; I had taken a loathing to my bed. How greatly I should have preferred the barn!

Game was plentiful that year; rabbits, hares, pheasants succeeded each other. After three evenings, Bute, seeing that everything was going so well, took it into his head to join us.

On the sixth of our poaching expeditions, we found only two of the twelve snares we had set; somebody had made a clearance during the daytime. Bute asked me for five francs to buy some more copper wire, as ordinary wire was no use.

The next morning I had the gratification of seeing my ten snares at Bocage's house and I was obliged to compliment him on his zeal. What annoyed me most was that the year before I had foolishly offered fifty centimes for every snare that was brought in; I had therefore to give Bocage five francs. In the meantime Bute had bought some more wire with the five francs

I had given him. Four days later, the same story! Ten fresh snares were brought in; another five francs to Bute; another five francs to Bocage. And as I congratulated him:

'It's not me you must congratulate, Sir, it's Alcide,' he said.

'No, really?' said I. Too much astonishment might have given me away. I controlled myself.

'Yes,' went on Bocage; 'it can't be helped, Sir, I'm growing old. The lad looks around the woods instead of me; he knows them very well; he can tell better than I can where to look out for the snares.'

'I'm sure he can, Bocage.'

'So out of the fifty centimes you give me, I let him have twenty-five.'

'He certainly deserves it. What! Twenty snares in five days! Excellent work! The poachers had better be careful. I wager they'll lie low now.'

'Oh, no, Sir. The more one takes, the more one finds. Game is very dear this year, and for the few sous it costs them . . .'

I had been so completely diddled that I felt almost inclined to suspect old Bocage himself of having a hand in the game. And what specially vexed me in the business was not so much Alcide's threefold traffic as his deceitfulness. And then what did he and Bute do with the money? I didn't know. I should never know anything about creatures like them. They would always lie; they would go on deceiving me for the sake of deceiving. That evening I gave Bute ten francs instead of five and warned him it was for the last time, that if the snares were taken again, so much the worse, but I should not go on.

The next day up came Bocage; he looked embarrassed – which at once made me feel even more so. What
had happened? Bocage told me that Bute had been out
all night and had only come in at cockcrow. The fellow
was as drunk as a fiddler; at Bocage's first words, he
had grossly insulted him and then flown at him and
struck him . . .

'And I've come to ask, Sir,' said Bocage, 'whether
you authorize me' (he accented the word a little),
'whether you *authorize* me to dismiss him?'

'I'll think about it, Bocage. I'm extremely sorry he
should have been disrespectful. I'll see . . . Let me
reflect a little and come again in two hours' time.'

Bocage went out.

To keep Bute was to be painfully lacking in consideration for Bocage; to dismiss Bute was to ask for
trouble. Well! there was nothing to be done about it.
Let come what come might! I had only myself to
blame . . . And as soon as Bocage came back:

'You can tell Bute we have no further use for him
here,' I said.

Then I waited. What would Bocage do? What would
Bute say? It was not till evening that I heard rumours
of scandal. Bute had spoken. I guessed it at first from
the shrieks I heard coming from Bocage's house; it
was Alcide being beaten. Bocage would soon be coming up to see me; here he was; I heard his old footsteps
approaching and my heart beat even faster than when I
was poaching. It was an intolerable moment. I should
have to trot out a lot of fine sentiments. I should be
obliged to take him seriously. What could I invent to
explain things? How badly I should act! I would have
given anything to throw up my part! Bocage came in. I

understood absolutely nothing of what he was saying. It was absurd; I had to make him begin all over again. In the end, this is what I made out. He thought that Bute was the only guilty party; the inconceivable truth had escaped him – that I could have given Bute ten francs! What for? He was too much of a Normandy peasant to admit the possibility of such a thing. Bute must have stolen those ten francs. Not a doubt of it! When he said I had given them to him, he was merely adding a lie to a theft; it was a mere invention to explain away his theft; Bocage wasn't the man to believe a trumped-up story like that ... There was no more talk of poaching. If Bocage had beaten Alcide, it was only because the boy had spent the night out.

So then, I am saved! In Bocage's eyes, at any rate, everything is all right. What a fool that fellow Bute is! This evening, I must say, I don't feel much inclined to go out poaching.

I thought that everything was all over, when an hour later in came Charles. He looked far from amiable; the bare sight of him was enough; he struck me as even more tedious than his father. To think that last year! ...

'Well, Charles! I haven't seen you for ever so long!'

'If you had wanted to see me, Sir, you had only to come down to the farm. You won't find *me* gallivanting about the woods at night.'

'Oh, your father has told you ...'

'My father has told me nothing, because my father knows nothing. What's the use of telling him at his age that his master is making a fool of him?'

'Take care, Charles, you're going too far ...'

'Oh, all right! You're the master – you can do as you please.'

'Charles, you know perfectly well I've made a fool of no one, and if I do as I please, it's because it does no one any harm but myself.'

He shrugged his shoulders slightly.

'How can one defend your interests when you attack them yourself? You can't protect both the keeper and the poacher at the same time.'

'Why not?'

'Because . . . Oh, you're a bit too clever for me, Sir, I just don't like to see my master joining up with rogues and undoing the work that other people do for him.'

Charles spoke with more and more confidence as he went on. He held himself almost with dignity. I noticed he had cut off his whiskers. For that matter, what he said was sensible enough, and as I kept silence (what could I have said?), he went on:

'You taught me last year, Sir, that one had duties to one's possessions. One ought to take one's duties seriously and not play with them . . . or else one doesn't deserve to have possessions.'

Silence.

'Is that all you have to say?'

'For this evening, yes, Sir; but if you ask me some other time, Sir, I may perhaps tell you that my father and I are leaving La Morinière.'

And he went out, bowing very low. I hardly took time to reflect:

'Charles! . . . He's right, by Jove! . . . Oh, if that's what's meant by possessions . . . Charles!' And I ran after him, caught up with him in the dark and called out hastily, as if in a hurry to clinch my sudden determination:

'You can tell your father that I am putting La Mor-inière up for sale.'

Charles bowed again gravely and went away without a word.

The whole thing is absurd! Absurd!

That evening, Marceline was not able to come down to dinner and sent word to say she was unwell. Full of anxiety, I hurried up to her room. She reassured me quickly. 'It's nothing but a cold,' she said. She thought she had caught a chill.

'Couldn't you have put on something warmer?'

'I put my shawl on the first moment I felt a shiver.'

'You should have put it on before you felt a shiver, not after.'

She looked at me and tried to smile ... Oh, perhaps it was because the day had begun so badly that I felt so anguished. If she had said aloud, 'Do you really care whether I live or not?' I should not have heard the words more clearly.

'Oh,' I thought, 'without a doubt, everything in my life is falling to pieces. Nothing that my hand grasps can my hand hold.'

I sprang to Marceline and covered her pale face with kisses. At that, she broke down and fell sobbing on my shoulder ...

'Oh, Marceline! Marceline! Let us go away. Any-where else but here I shall love you as I did at Sorrento ... You have thought me changed, perhaps? But any-where else, you will feel that there is nothing altered in our love.'

I had not cured her unhappiness, but how eagerly she clutched at hope! ...

It was not late in the year, but the weather was cold

and damp, and the last rosebuds were rotting unopened on the bushes. Our guests had long since left us. Marceline was not too unwell to see to the shutting up of the house, and five days later we left.

THIRD PART

I

AND so I tried, yet once more, to close my hand over my love. But what did I want with peaceful happiness? What Marceline gave me, what she stood for in my eyes, was like rest to a man who is not tired. But as I felt she was weary and needed my love, I showered it upon her and pretended that the need was mine. I felt her sufferings unbearably; it was to cure her that I loved her.

O days and nights of passionate tender care! As others stimulate their faith by exaggerating the observance of its practices, so I fanned my love. And Marceline, as I tell you, began forthwith to recover hope. In her there was still so much youth; in me, she thought, so much promise.

We fled from Paris, as though for another honeymoon. But on the very first day of the journey, she got much worse and we had to break it at Neuchâtel.

I loved this lake, which had nothing Alpine about it, with its grey-green shores, and its waters mingling for a long space, marsh-like, with the land, and filtering through the rushes. I found a very comfortable hotel, with a room looking on to the lake for Marceline. I stayed with her the whole day.

She was so far from well the next day that I sent for a doctor from Lausanne. He wanted to know, quite uselessly, whether there were any other cases of tuberculosis in my wife's family. I said there were, though, as a matter of fact, I knew of none; but I disliked saying that I myself had been almost given up on account of it, and that Marceline had never been ill before she nursed me. I put the whole thing down to the score of the clot, though the doctor declared that this was merely a contributory cause and that the trouble dated from further back. He strongly recommended the air of the high Alps, which he assured me would cure her; and as just what I myself wished was to spend the whole winter in the Engadine, we started as soon as she was able to bear the journey.

I remember every sensation of that journey as vividly as if they had been events. The weather was limpid and cold; we had taken our warmest furs with us ... At Coire, the incessant din in the hotel almost entirely prevented us from sleeping. I myself should have put up cheerfully with a sleepless night and not found it tiring; but Marceline ... And it was not so much the noise that irritated me as the fact that she was not able to sleep in spite of it. Her need of sleep was so great! The next morning we started before daybreak; we had taken places in the coupé of the Coire diligence; the relays were so arranged that Saint-Moritz could be reached in one day.

Tiefenkasten, the Julier, Samaden ... I remember it all, hour by hour; I remember the strange, inclement feeling of the air; the sound of the horses' bells; my hunger; the midday halt at the inn; the raw egg that I broke into my soup; the brown bread and the sour wine that was so cold. This coarse fare did not suit Marceline; she could eat hardly anything but a few dry biscuits, which I had had the forethought to bring with me. I can recall the closing in of the daylight; the swiftness with which the shade climbs up the wooded mountainside; then another halt. And now the air becomes keener, rawer. When the coach stops, we plunge into the heart of darkness, into a silence that is limpid – limpid – there is no other word for it. The quality, the sonority of the slightest sound acquire perfection and fullness in that strange transparency. Another start – in the night, this time. Marceline coughs ... Oh, will she never have done coughing? I think of the Sousse diligence; I feel as if I had coughed better than that. She makes too great an effort ... How weak and changed she looks! In the shadow there, I should hardly recognize her. How drawn her features are! Used those two black holes of her nostrils always to be so visible? ... Oh, how horribly she is coughing! Is that the best she can do? I have a horror of sympathy. It is the lurking place of every kind of contagion; one ought only to sympathize with the strong. Oh! she seems really at the last gasp. Shall we never arrive? What is she doing now? She takes her handkerchief out, puts it to her lips, turns aside ... Horror! Is she going to spit blood too? I snatch the handkerchief roughly from her hand, and in the half light of the lantern look at it ... Nothing. But my anxiety has been too visible. Marceline attempts a melancholy smile and murmurs:

'No; not yet.'

At last we arrived. It was time, for she could hardly stand. I did not like the rooms that had been prepared for us; we spent the night in them however, and changed them the next day. Nothing seemed fine enough for me nor too expensive. And as the winter season had not yet begun, the vast hotel was almost empty and I was able to choose. I took two spacious rooms, bright, and simply furnished; there was a large sitting-room adjoining, with a big bow-window, from which could be seen the hideous blue lake and a crude mountain, whose name I have forgotten and whose slopes were either too wooded or too bare. We had our meals served separately. The rooms were extravagantly dear. But what do I care? I thought. It is true I no longer have my lectures, but I am selling La Morinière. And then we shall see ... Besides, what need have I of money? What need have I of all this? ... I am strong now ... A complete change of fortune, I think, must be as instructive as a complete change of health ... Marceline, of course, requires luxury; she is weak ... oh, for her sake, I will spend so much, so much that ... And I felt at one and the same time a horror of luxury and a craving for it. I bathed, I steeped my sensuality in it, and then again it was a vagabond joy that I longed for.

In the meanwhile Marceline was getting better and my constant care was having good results. As she had a difficulty in eating, I ordered the most dainty and delicious food to stimulate her appetite; we drank the best wines. The foreign brands we experimented on every day amused me so much that I persuaded myself she had a great fancy for them; sharp Rhine wines, almost syrupy Tokays, that filled me with their heady virtue. I remember too an extraordinary Barba-grisca, of which only one bottle was left, so that I never knew whether the others would have had the same bizarre taste.

Every day we went for a drive, first in a carriage, and later on, when the snow had fallen, in a sledge, wrapped up to our eyes in fur. I came in with glowing cheeks, hungry and then sleepy. I had not, however, given up all idea of work, and every day I found an hour or so in which to meditate on the things I felt it was my duty to say. There was no question of history now; I had long since ceased to take any interest in historical studies except as a means of psychological investigation. I have told you how I had been attracted afresh to the past when I thought I could see in it a disquieting resemblance to the present; I had actually dared to think that by questioning the dead I should be able to extort from them some secret information about life ... But now if the youthful Athalaric himself had risen from the grave to speak to me, I should not have listened to him. How could the ancient past have answered my present question? – What can man do more? that is what seemed to me important to know. Is what man has hitherto said all that he *could* say? Is there nothing in himself he has overlooked? Can he do nothing but repeat himself? ... And every day there grew stronger in me a confused consciousness of untouched treasures somewhere lying covered up, hidden, smothered by culture and decency and morality.

It seemed to me then that I had been born to make discoveries of a kind hitherto undreamed of; and I grew strangely and passionately eager in the pursuit of my dark and mysterious researches, for the sake of which, I well knew, the searcher must abjure and repudiate culture and decency and morality.

I soon went to the length of sympathizing only with the wildest outbreaks of conduct in other people, and of regretting that such manifestations were subject to any control whatever. I came very near thinking that honesty was merely the result of restrictions or conventions or fear. I should have liked to cherish it as something rare and difficult; but our manners had turned it into a form of mutual advantage and commonplace contract. In Switzerland, it is just a part of one's comfort. I understood that Marceline required it; but I did not conceal from her the new trend of my thoughts; as early as Neuchâtel, when she was praising the honesty that is so visible in the faces of the people and the walls of the houses.

'I prefer my own,' I retorted. 'I have a horror of honest folk. I may have nothing to fear from them, but I have nothing to learn either. And besides, they have nothing to say ... Honest Swiss nation! What does their health do for them? They have neither crimes, nor history, not literature, nor arts ... a hardy rose-tree, without thorns or flowers.'

That I should be bored by this honest country was a foregone conclusion, but at the end of two months, my boredom became a kind of frenzy and my one thought was to fly.

We were in the middle of January, Marceline was better – much better; the continual low fever that was undermining her had disappeared; a brighter colour had returned to her cheeks; she once more enjoyed walking, though not for long, and was not continually tired as she used to be. I did not have much difficulty in persuading her that the bracing air had done her all the good that could be expected and that the best thing for her now would be to go down into Italy, where the kindly warmth of spring would completely restore her ... and above all, I had not much difficulty in persuading myself – so utterly sick was I of those mountain heights.

And yet now, when in my idleness the detested past once more asserts its strength, those are the very memories that haunt me. Swift sledge drives; joy of the dry and stinging air, spattering of the snow, appetite; walks in the baffling fog, curious sonority of voices, abrupt appearance of objects; readings in the snug warmth of the sitting-room, view of the landscape through the windows, view of the icy landscape; tragic waiting for the snow; vanishing of the outer world, soft brooding of one's thoughts ... Oh, to skate with her alone once more on the little lake, lying lost among the larches, pure and peaceful – oh, to come home with her once more at night! ...

That descent into Italy gave me all the dizzy sensations of a fall. The weather was fine. As we dropped into a warmer and denser air, the rigid trees of the highlands – the larches and symmetrical fir-trees – gave way to the softness, the grace and ease of a luxurious vegetation. I felt I was leaving abstraction for life, and though it was winter, I imagined perfumes in every breath. Oh, for long – too long, our only smiles had been for shadows! My abstemiousness had gone to my head and I was drunk with thirst as others are with wine. My thrift of life had been admirable; on the threshold of this land of tolerance and promise, all my appetites broke out with sudden vehemence. I was full to bursting with an immense reserve of love; sometimes it surged from the obscure depths of my senses up into my head and turned my thoughts to shamelessness.

This illusion of spring did not last long. The sudden change of altitude may have deceived me for a moment, but as soon as we left the sheltered shores of the lakes, Bellagio and Como, where we lingered for a day or two, we came into winter and rain. We now suffered from the cold, which we had borne well enough in the Engadine; it was not dry and exhilarating here as it had been in the mountains, but damp and heavy, and Marceline began to cough again. In order to escape it, we pursued our way still further south; we left Milan for Florence, Florence for Rome, Rome for Naples, which in the winter rain is really the most lugubrious town I know. I dragged along in unspeakable ennui. We went back to Rome in the hopes of finding, if not warmth, at least a semblance of comfort. We rented an apartment on the Pincio, much too vast, but marvellously situated. Already, at Florence, disgusted with hotels, we had rented a lovely villa on the Viale dei Colli, for three months. Anybody else would have wished to spend a lifetime in it ... We stayed barely three weeks. And yet at every fresh stage, I made a point of arranging everything as if we were never going to leave ... Some irresistible demon goaded me on ... And add to this that we travelled with no fewer than eight trunks. There was one I never opened during the whole journey, entirely filled with books.

I did not allow Marceline to have any say in our expenses or attempt to moderate them. I knew of course that they were excessive and that they could not last. I could no longer count on any money from La Morinière. It had ceased to bring in anything, and Bocage wrote that he could not find a purchaser. But all thoughts of the future ended only in making me spend the more. What need should I have of so much money, once I was alone, I thought; and sick at heart, I watched

Marceline's frail life as it ebbed away more quickly still than my fortune.

Although she depended on me for all the arrangements, these perpetual and hurried moves tired her; but what tired her still more (I do not hesitate now to acknowledge it) was the fear of what was in my mind.

'I understand,' she said to me one day, 'I quite understand your doctrine – for now it has become a doctrine. A fine one perhaps,' and then she added sadly, dropping her voice, 'but it does away with the weak.'

'And so it should!' was the answer that burst from me in spite of myself.

In my heart then, I felt the sensitive creature shiver and shrivel up at the shock of my dreadful words . . . Oh, perhaps you will think I did not love Marceline. I swear I loved her passionately. She had never been – I had never thought her – so beautiful. Illness had refined – etherealized her features. I hardly ever left her, surrounded her with every care, watched over her every moment of the night and day. If she slept lightly, I trained myself to sleep more lightly still; I watched her as she fell asleep and I was the first to wake. When sometimes I left her for an hour to take a solitary walk in the country or streets, a kind of loving anxiety, a fear of her feeling the time long, made me hurry back to her; and sometimes I rebelled against this obsession, called upon my will to help me against it, said to myself, 'Are you worth no more than this, you make-believe great man?' And I forced myself to prolong my absence; but then I would come in, my arms laden with flowers, early garden flowers, or hothouse blooms . . . Yes, I say; I cared for her tenderly. But how can I express this – that in proportion as I respected myself less, I revered her more? And who shall say how many passions and how many hostile thoughts may live together in the mind of man? ...

The bad weather had long since ceased; the season was advancing; and suddenly the almond trees were in bloom. The day was the first of March. I went down in the morning to the Piazza di Spagna. The peasants had stripped the Campagna of its white branches, and the flower-sellers' baskets were full of almond blossom. I was so enchanted that I bought a whole grove of it. Three men carried it for me. I went home with all this flowering spring. The branches caught on the doorways and petals snowed upon the carpet. I put the blossoms everywhere, filled all the vases, and, while Marceline was absent from the drawing-room for a moment, made it a bower of whiteness. I was already picturing her delight, when I heard her step ...! She opened the door. Oh, what was wrong with her? ... She tottered ... She burst out sobbing.

'What is it, my poor Marceline?' ...

I ran up to her, showered the tenderest caresses upon her. Then as if to excuse her tears:

'The flowers smell too strong,' she said ...

And it was a faint, faint, exquisite scent of honey. ... Without a word, I seized the innocent fragile branches, broke them to pieces, carried them out of the room and flung them away, my temples throbbing with exasperation, my nerves ajar. Oh, if she finds this little bit of spring too much for her! ...

I have often thought over those tears of hers and I believe now that she already felt herself condemned and was crying for the loss of other springs ... I think too that there are strong joys for the strong and weak joys for the weak who would be hurt by strong joys. She was sated by the merest trifle of pleasure; one shade brighter and it was more than she could bear. What she called happiness, I called rest, and I was unwilling, unable to rest.

Four days later we left again for Sorrento. I was disappointed not to find it warmer. The whole country seemed shivering with cold. The wind, which never ceased blowing, was a severe trial to Marceline. Our plan was to go to the same hotel we had been at the time of our first journey, and we were given the same room ... But how astonished we were to see that the grey sky had robbed the whole scene of its magic, and that the place we had thought so charming when we had walked in it as lovers was nothing but a dreary hotel garden!

We settled then to go by sea to Palermo, whose climate we had heard praised; we returned therefore to Naples, where we were to take the boat and where we stayed on for a few days longer. But at any rate, I was not dull at Naples. Naples is alive – a town that is not overshadowed by the past.

I spent nearly every moment of the day with Marceline. At night she was tired and went to bed early; I watched by her until she went to sleep and sometimes went to bed myself; then, when her more regular breathing told me she was asleep, I got up again noiselessly, dressed in the dark, slipped out of door like a thief.

Out of doors! Oh, I could have shouted with joy! What was I bent on? I cannot tell. The sky, which had been dark all day, was cleared of its clouds; the moon was nearly full. I walked at random, without object, without desire, without constraint. I looked at everything with a fresh eye; I listened to every noise with an attentive ear; I breathed the dampness of the night; I touched things with my hand; I went prowling.

The last night we spent at Naples I stayed out later than usual on this vagabond debauch. When I came in, I found Marceline in tears. She had waked up suddenly, she said, and been frightened at not feeling me there. I calmed her, explained my absence as well as I could, and resolved not to leave her again. But the first night we spent at Palermo was too much for me – I went out. The orange trees were in flower; the slightest breath of air came laden with their scent . . .

We only stayed five days at Palermo; then, by a long detour, we made our way to Taormina, which we both wanted to see again. I think I have told you that the village is perched high on the mountain side; the station is on the seashore. The carriage that drove us to the hotel took me back again to the station for me to get our trunks. I stood up in the carriage in order to talk to the driver. He was a Sicilian boy from Catania, as beautiful as a line of Theocritus, full of colour, and odour and savour, like a fruit.

'*Com'è bella, la signora!*' said he, in a charming voice, as he watched Marceline go into the hotel.

'*Anche tu sei bello, ragazzo,*' I replied; then, as I was standing so near him, I could not resist, but drew him to me and kissed him. He allowed it laughingly.

'*I Francesi sono tutti amanti,*' he said.

'*Ma non tutti gli Italiani amati,*' I answered, laughing too . . . I looked for him on the following days, but never succeeded in finding him.

We left Taormina for Syracuse. Step by step we went over the ground we had covered in our first journey, making our way back to the starting point of our love. And as during our first journey I had week by week progressed towards recovery, so week by week as we went southwards, Marceline's health grew worse.

By what aberration, what obstinate blindness, what deliberate folly did I persuade myself, did I above all try and persuade her that what she wanted was still more light and warmth? Why did I remind her of my convalescence at Biskra? ... And yet the air had become warmer; the climate of Palermo is mild and pleasant; Marceline liked it. There, perhaps, she might have ... But had I the power to choose what I should determine – to decide what I should desire? The state of the sea and the irregular boat-service delayed us a week at Syracuse. All the time I did not spend with Marceline I spent in the old port. O little port of Syracuse! Smells of sour wine, muddy alleys, stinking booths, where dockers and vagabonds and wine-bibbing sailors loaf and jostle! The society of the lowest dregs of humanity was delectable company to me. And what need had I to understand their language, when I felt it in my whole body? Even the brutality of their passion assumed in my eyes a hypocritical appearance of health and vigour. In vain I told myself that their wretched life could not have the same flavour for them that it had for me ... Oh, I wished I could have rolled under the table with them to wake up only with the first grey shiver of dawn. And their company whetted my growing horror of luxury, of comfort, of all the things I was wrapped round with, of the protection that my newly restored health had made unnecessary, of all the precautions one takes to preserve one's body from the perilous contact of life. I imagined their existence in other surroundings. I should have liked to follow them elsewhere, to probe deeper into their drunken life ... Then suddenly I thought of Marceline. What was she doing at this very moment? Suffering, crying, perhaps ... I got up hastily and hurried back to the hotel; there, over the door, seemed written the words: No poor admitted here.

Marceline always received me in the same way, without a word of reproach or suspicion, and struggling, in spite of everything, to smile. We took our meals in private; I ordered for her the best our very second-rate hotel could provide. And all through the meal, I kept thinking, 'A piece of bread, a bit of cheese, a head of fennel is enough for *them* and would be enough for *me* too. And perhaps out there, close by, some of them are hungry and have not even that wretched pittance. And here on my table is enough to fill them for three days.' I should have liked to break down the walls and let the guests flock in ... For to feel there were people suffering from hunger was dreadful. And I went back again to the port and scattered about at random the small coins with which my pockets were filled.

Poverty is a slave-driver; in return for food, men give their grudging labour; all work that is not joyous is wretched, I thought, and I paid many of them to rest. 'Don't work,' I said, 'you hate it.' In imagination, I bestowed on each of them that leisure without which nothing can blossom – neither vice nor art.

Marceline did not mistake my thoughts; when I came back from the port, I did not conceal from her what sort of wretches I had been frequenting. Every kind of thing goes to the making of a man. Marceline knew well enough what I was trying so furiously to discover; and as I reproached her for being too apt to credit everyone she knew with special virtues of her own invention. 'You,' said she, 'are never satisfied until you have made people exhibit some vice. Don't you understand that by looking at any particular trait, we develop and exaggerate it? And that we make a man become what we think him?'

I could have wished she were wrong, but I had to admit that the worst instinct of every human being appeared to me the sincerest. But then what did I mean by sincere?

We left Syracuse at last. I was haunted by the desire and the memory of the past. At sea, Marceline's health improved ... I can still see the colour of the sea. It is so calm that the ship's track in it seems permanent. I can still hear the noises of dripping and dropping water – liquid noises; the swabbing of the deck and the slapping of the sailors' bare feet on the boards. I can see Malta shining white in the sun – the approach to Tunis ... How changed I am!

It was hot; it was fine; everything was glorious. Oh, how I wish that every one of my sentences here could distill a quintessence of voluptuous delight! ... I cannot hope to tell my story now with more order than I lived my life. I have been long enough trying to explain how I became what I am. Oh, if only I could rid my mind of all this intolerable logic! ... I feel I have nothing in me that is not noble.

Tunis! The quality of the light here is not strength but abundance. The shade is still full of it. The air itself is like a luminous fluid in which everything is steeped; one bathes, one swims in it. This land of pleasure satisfies desire without appeasing it, and desire is sharpened by satisfaction.

A land free from works of art; I despise those who cannot recognize beauty until it has been transcribed and interpreted. The Arabs have this admirable quality, that they live their art, sing it, dissipate it from day to day; is it not fixed, not embalmed in any work. This is the cause and effect of the absence of great artists ... I have always thought that great artists were those who dared to confer the right of beauty on things so natural that people say on seeing them, 'Why did I never realize before that that was beautiful too?'

At Kairouan, which I had not seen before, and which I visited without Marceline, the night was very fine. As I was going back to sleep at the hotel, I remembered a group of Arabs I had seen lying out of doors on mats, outside a little café. I went and lay down to sleep beside them. I came away covered with vermin.

Marceline found the damp of the coast very enfeebling, and I persuaded her that we ought to go on to Biskra as quickly as possible. We were now at the beginning of April.

The journey to Biskra is a very long one. The first day we went to Constantine without a break; the second day, Marceline was very tired and we only got as far as El Kantara. I remember seeking there, and towards evening finding, shade that was more delicious and cool than moonshine at night. It flowed about us like a stream of inexhaustible refreshment. And from

148

the bank where we were sitting we could see the plain aflame in the setting sun. That night Marceline could not sleep, disturbed as she was by the strange silence or the tiniest of noises. I was afraid she was feverish. I heard her tossing in the night. Next morning I thought she looked paler. We went on again.

Biskra! That then was my goal ... Yes; there are the public gardens; the bench ... I recognize the bench on which I used to sit in the first days of my convalescence. What was it I read there? ... Homer; I have not opened the book since. There is the tree with the curious bark I got up to go and feel. How weak I was then! Look! there come some children! ... No; I recognize none of them. How grave Marceline is! She is as changed as I. Why does she cough so in this fine weather? There is the hotel! There are our rooms, our terrace! What is Marceline thinking? She has not said a word. As soon as she gets to her room she lies down on the bed; she is tired and says she wants to sleep a little. I go out.

I do not recognize the children, but the children recognize me. They have heard of my arrival and come running to meet me. Can it really be they? What a shock! What has happened? They have grown out of all knowledge – hideously. In barely two years! It seems impossible ... What fatigues, what vices, what sloth have put their ugly mark on faces that were once so bright with youth? What vile labours can so soon have stunted those beautiful young limbs? What a bankruptcy of hope! ... I ask a few questions. Bachir is scullion in a café; Ashour is laboriously earning a few pennies by breaking stones on the roads; Hammatar has lost an eye. And who would believe it?

Sadek has settled down! He helps an elder brother sell loaves in the market; he looks idiotic. Agib has set up as a butcher with his father; he is getting fat; he is ugly; he is rich; he refuses to speak to his low-class companions ... How stupid honourable careers make people! What! Am I going to find here the same things I hated so at home? Boubakir? Married. He is not fifteen yet. It is grotesque. Not altogether though. When I see him that evening he explains that his marriage is a mere farce. He is, I expect, an utter waster; he has taken to drink and lost his looks ... So that is all that remains, is it? That is what life has made of them? My intolerable depression makes me feel it was largely to see them that I came here. Ménalque was right. Memory is an accursed invention.

And Moktir? Ah! Moktir has just come out of prison. He is lying low. The others will have nothing to do with him. I want to see him. He used to be the handsomest of them all. Is he to be a disappointment too? ... Someone finds him out and brings him to me. No; Moktir has not failed. Even my memory had not painted him as superb as he now is. His strength, his beauty are flawless ... He smiles as he recognizes me.

'And what did you do before you went to prison?'
'Nothing.'
'Did you steal?'
He protests.
'And what are you doing now?'
He smiles.
'Well, Moktir, if you have nothing to do, you must come with us to Touggourt.' And I suddenly feel seized with a desire to go to Touggourt.

Marceline is not well; I do not know what is going

on in her mind. When I go back to the hotel that evening, she presses up against me without saying a word and without opening her eyes. Her wide sleeve has slipped up and shows how thin she has grown. I take her in my arms, as if she were a sleepy child, and rock and soothe her. Is it love, or anguish or fever that makes her tremble so? ... Oh! perhaps there might still be time ... Will nothing make me stop? ... I know now – I have found out at last what gives me my special value. It is a kind of stubborn perseverance in evil. But how do I bring myself to tell Marceline that next day we are to leave again for Touggourt? ...

She is asleep now in the room next mine. The moon has been up some time and is flooding the terrace. The brightness is almost terrifying. There is no hiding from it. The floor of my room is tiled with white, and there the light is brightest. It streams through the wide-open window. I recognize the way it shines into the room and the shadow made by the door. Two years ago, it came in still further ... Yes; it is almost at the same spot it had reached that night I got up because I could not sleep ... It was against that very door-jamb I leaned my shoulder. I recognize the stillness of the palm-trees. What was the sentence I read that night? ... Oh, yes; Christ's words to Peter: 'Now thou girdest thyself and goest where thou wouldest ...' Where am I going? Where would I go? ... I did not tell you that the last time I was at Naples, I went to Paestum one day by myself. Oh, I could have wept at the sight of those ruined stones. The ancient beauty shone out from them, simple, perfect, smiling – deserted. Art is leaving me, I feel it. To make room for what else? The smiling harmony once mine is mine no longer ... No

longer do I know what dark mysterious God I serve.
O great new God! grant me the knowledge of other
newer races, unimagined types of beauty.

The next morning at daybreak, we left in the diligence, and Moktir came with us. Moktir was as happy
as a king.

Chegga; Kefeldorh'; M'reyer ... dreary stages of a
still more dreary road – an interminable road. I confess
I had expected these oases to be more smiling. But
there is nothing here but stone and sand; at times a few
shrubs with queer flowers; at times an attempt at palm-
trees, watered by some hidden spring ... Now, to any
oasis, I prefer the desert – land of mortal glory and intolerable splendour! Man's effort here seems ugly and
miserable. All other lands now are weariness to me.

'You like what is inhuman,' says Marceline.

But she herself, how greedily she looks!

Next day it was not so fine; that is, a wind sprang up
and the horizon became dull and grey.

Marceline is suffering; the sand in the air burns and
irritates her throat; the overabundance of light tires
her eyes; the hostile landscape crushes her. But it is too
late now to turn back. In a few hours we shall be at
Touggourt.

It is this last part of the journey, though it is still so
near me, that I remember least. I find it impossible to
recall the scenery of the second day or what I did when
we first got to Touggourt. But what I do still remember
are my impatience and my haste.

It had been very cold that morning. Towards evening a burning simoon sprang up. Marceline, exhausted
by the journey, went to bed as soon as we arrived. I had
hoped to find a rather more comfortable hotel, but our

room is hideous; the sand, the sun, the flies have tarnished, dirtied, discoloured everything. As we have eaten scarcely anything since daybreak, I order a meal to be served at once; but Marceline finds everything uneatable and I cannot persuade her to touch a morsel. We have with us paraphernalia for making our own tea. I attend to this trifling business, and for dinner we content ourselves with a few biscuits and the tea, made with the brackish water of the country and tasting horrible in consequence.

By a last semblance of virtue, I stay with her till evening. And all of a sudden I feel that I myself have come to the end of my strength. O. taste of ashes! O deadly lassitude! O the sadness of superhuman effort! I hardly dare look at her; I am too certain that my eyes, instead of seeking hers, will fasten horribly on the black holes of her nostrils; the suffering expression of her face is agonizing. Nor does she look at me either. I feel her anguish as if I could touch it. She coughs a great deal and then falls asleep. From time to time, she is shaken by a sudden shudder.

Perhaps the night will be bad, and before it is too late I must find out where I can get help. I go out.

Outside the hotel, the Touggourt square, the streets, the very atmosphere, are so strange that I can hardly believe it is I who see them. After a little I go in again. Marceline is sleeping quietly. I need not have been so frightened; in this peculiar country, one suspects peril everywhere. Absurd! And more or less reassured, I again go out.

There is a strange nocturnal animation in the square – a silent flitting to and fro – a stealthy gliding of white burnouses. The wind at times tears off a shred of strange music and brings it from I know not where. Someone comes up to me ... Moktir! He was waiting for me, he says – expected me to come out again. He laughs. He knows Touggourt, comes here often, knows where to take me. I let myself be guided by him.

We walk along in the dark and go into a Moorish café; this is where the music came from. Some Arab women are dancing – if such a monotonous glide can be called dancing. One of them takes me by the hand; I follow her; she is Moktir's mistress; he comes too ... We all three go into the deep, narrow room where the only piece of furniture is a bed ... A very low bed on which we sit down. A white rabbit which has been shut up in the room is scared at first but afterwards grows tamer and comes to feed out of Moktir's hand. Coffee is brought. Then, while Moktir is playing with the rabbit, the woman draws me towards her, and I let myself go to her as one lets oneself sink into sleep ...

Oh, here I might deceive you or be silent – but what use can this story be to me, if it ceases to be truthful?

I go back alone to the hotel, for Moktir remains behind in the café. It is late. A parching sirocco is blowing; the wind is laden with sand, and, in spite of the night, torrid. After three or four steps, I am bathed in sweat; but I suddenly feel I must hurry and I reach the hotel almost at a run. She is awake perhaps ... Perhaps she wants me? ... No; the window of her room is dark. I wait for a short lull in the wind before opening the door; I go into the room very softly in the dark. What is that noise? ... I do not recognize her cough ... Is it really Marceline? ... I light the light.

She is half sitting on the bed, one of her thin arms clutching the bars and supporting her in an upright position; her sheets, her hands, her nightdress are flooded with a stream of blood; her face is soiled with it; her eyes have grown hideously big; and no cry of agony could be more appalling than her silence. Her face is bathed in sweat; I try to find a little place on it where I can put a horrible kiss; I feel the taste of her sweat on my lips. I wash and refresh her forehead and cheeks ... What is that hard thing I feel under my foot near the bed? I stoop down and pick up the little rosary that she once asked for in Paris and which she has dropped on the ground. I slip it over her open hand, but immediately she lowers her hand and drops the rosary again ... What am I to do? I wish I could get help ... Her hand clutches me desperately, holds me tight; oh, can she think I want to leave her? She says:

'Oh, you can wait a little longer, can't you?' Then, as she sees I want to say something.

'Don't speak,' she adds; 'everything is all right.'

I pick up the rosary again and put it back on her hand, but again she lets it drop – yes, deliberately – lets it drop. I kneel down beside her, take her hand, and press it to me.

She lets herself go, partly against the pillow, partly against my shoulder, seems to sleep a little, but her eyes are still wide open.

An hour later, she raises herself, disengages her hand from mine, clutches at her nightdress, and tears the lace. She is choking.

Towards morning she had another haemorrhage ...

*

I have finished telling you my story. What more should I say?

The French cemetery at Touggourt is a hideous place, half devoured by the sand ... What little energy I had left I spent in carrying her away from that miserable spot. She rests at El Kantara, in the shade of a private garden she liked. It all happened barely three months ago. Those three months have put a distance of ten years between that time and this.

MICHEL *remained silent for a long time. We did not speak either, for we each of us had a strange feeling of uneasiness. We felt, alas, that by telling his story, Michel had made his action more legitimate. Our not having known at what point to condemn it in the course of his long explanation seemed almost to make us his accomplices. We felt, as it were, involved. He finished his story without a quaver in his voice, without an inflection or a gesture to show that he was feeling any emotion whatever; he might have had a cynical pride in not appearing moved or a kind of shyness that made him afraid of arousing emotion in us by his tears, or he might not in fact have been moved. Even now I cannot guess in what proportions pride, strength, reserve, and want of feeling were combined in him. After a pause he went on:*

'What frightens me, I admit, is that I am still very young. It seems to me sometimes that my real life has not begun. Take me away from here and give me some reason for living. I have none left. I have freed myself. That may be. But what does it signify? This objectless liberty is a burden to me. It is not, believe me, that I am tired of my crime – if you choose to call it that – but I must prove to myself that I have not overstepped my rights.

'When you knew me first, I had great stability of thought, and I know that that is what makes real men. I have it no longer. But I think it is the fault of this climate. Nothing is more discouraging to thought than this persistent azure. Enjoyment here follows so closely upon desire that effort is impossible. Here, in the midst of splendour and death, I feel the presence of happiness too close, the yielding to it too uniform. In the middle of the day, I go and lie down on my bed to while away the long dreary hours and their intolerable leisure.

'Look! I have here a number of white pebbles. I let them soak in the shade, then hold them in the hollow of my hand and wait until their soothing coolness is exhausted. Then I begin once more, changing the pebbles and putting back those that have lost their coolness to soak in the shade again ... Time passes and the evening comes on ... Take me away; I cannot move of myself. Something in my will is broken; I don't even know how I had the strength to leave El Kantara. Sometimes I am afraid that what I have suppressed will take vengeance on me. I should like to begin over again. I should like to get rid of the remains of my fortune; you see the walls here are still covered with it ... I live for next to nothing in this place. A half-caste innkeeper prepares what little food I need. The boy who ran away at your approach brings it to me in the evening and morning, in exchange for a few sous and a caress or two. He turns shy with strangers, but with me he is as affectionate and faithful as a dog. His sister is an Ouled-Naïl and in the winter goes back to Constantine to sell her body to the passers-by. She is very beautiful, and in the first weeks I sometimes allowed her to pass the night with me. But one morning, her brother, little Ali, surprised us together. He showed great annoyance and refused to come back for five days. And yet he knows perfectly well how and on what his sister lives; he used to speak of it before without the slightest embarrassment ... Can he be jealous? Be that as it may, the little rascal has succeeded in his object; for, partly from distaste, partly because I was afraid of losing Ali, I have given the woman up since this incident. She has not taken offence; but every time I meet her, she laughs and declares that I prefer the boy to her. She makes out that it is he who keeps me here. Perhaps she is not altogether wrong . . .'